"I don't blame her for acting out. She's lost everyone she loves," J.C. said.

Unexpectedly, Maddie covered his hand with hers. "Not quite everyone."

He stared at her long, slender fingers and pulled his gaze back to hers. "My niece has been fighting with some of the girls at school, her grades are slipping." And Chrissy was miserable.

Concern etched Maddie's face. "Can I help? She could spend afternoons with us."

"Don't have enough on your plate now?"

"It's what we do. You know, here in Rosewood. She's a child who needs any help we can give her."

It was how J.C. had been raised, too. "Maybe from people who have the time. You're exhausted now. I'm not going to add to that burden."

The fire in her now stormy gray eyes was one he remembered. "It's not a burden. I have enough energy to spare some for Chrissy."

She was pretty remarkable, J.C. decided. Even more remarkable—she didn't seem to realize it.

Books by Bonnie K. Winn

Love Inspired

*A Family All Her Own
*Family Ties
*Promise of Grace
*Protected Hearts
*Child of Mine
*To Love Again
*Lone Star Blessings
*Return to Rosewood
*Jingle Bell Blessings
*Family by Design

*Rosewood, Texas

BONNIE K. WINN

is a hopeless romantic who has written incessantly since the third grade. So it seems only natural that she turned to romance writing. A seasoned author of historical and contemporary romance, Bonnie has won numerous awards for her bestselling books. *Affaire de Coeur* chose her as one of the Top Ten Romance Writers in America.

Bonnie loves writing contemporary romance because she can set her stories in the modern cities close to her heart and explore the endlessly fascinating strengths of today's women.

Living in the foothills of the Rockies gives her plenty of inspiration and a touch of whimsy, as well. She shares her life with her husband, son and a spunky Norwich terrier who lends his characteristics to many pets in her stories. Bonnie's keeping mum about anyone else's characteristics she may have borrowed.

Family by Design
Bonnie K. Winn

Love Inspired

Recycling programs
for this product may
not exist in your area.

LOVE INSPIRED BOOKS

ISBN-13: 978-0-373-81565-4

FAMILY BY DESIGN

www.LoveInspiredBooks.com

Printed in U.S.A.

Many daughters have done nobly,
But you excel them all.
—*Proverbs* 31:29

For Erica Endo, daughter of my heart.

Chapter One

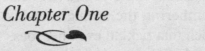

Maddie Carter forgot to breathe. Her hand, swallowed by the doctor's larger one, rioted in unexpected reaction.

Dr. J. C. Mueller smiled and she gaped, unable to think of anything coherent to say as he turned to her mother, Lillian.

"So, Mrs. Carter, I understand your G.P. recommended you meet with me." He winked. "Of course, I am the only neurologist in Rosewood."

Maddie stumbled on her way to the extra chair in the examining room, righting herself quickly, hoping he hadn't noticed.

How had she forgotten this man? True, he'd been three years ahead of her in high school, then he'd gone to Baylor, while she'd attended the University of Texas, but still… She couldn't stop staring. Tall, broad-shouldered, with a shock of thick dark hair, mesmerizing brown eyes and a cleft in his chin that begged to be touched.

J.C. flipped through the thick pile of pages in her mother's chart, detailing the history of strokes that had brought on early onset dementia. He put down the folder, picking up Lillian's hand, placing two fingers over her upturned wrist.

Maddie couldn't still her heartbeat, instantly remembering the strength of his long fingers, the touch that tickled even her toes.

"Mrs. Carter, your vital signs are excellent."

Pleased, Lillian smiled. "Thank you, young man."

"I'd like to run a few tests, nothing invasive."

"Have I met you before?" Lillian questioned, puzzled.

"I grew up here in Rosewood," J.C. responded patiently. His wide smile was easy, kind. And his gold-flecked brown eyes sparkled.

Maddie's own pulse increased. *Good thing he wasn't recording hers.*

"How about you, Mrs. Carter? Are you from Rosewood originally?"

Maddie recognized the pattern to the handsome doctor's questions. He wanted to see if her mother could remember and verbalize her recollections. Lillian's worsening symptoms had prompted their G.P.'s referral to a specialist.

"My mother was born here," Lillian mused, her pale blue eyes reflective. "My father came from the Panhandle, near Amarillo. But he took one look at her and knew he wanted to stay." Smiling, she looked up at the doctor. "Love will do that, you know."

"Yes, ma'am," J.C. agreed, stretching out his long legs.

Immediately, Maddie wondered if he was married, engaged. Surely some smart woman had snagged him long ago.

"So you raised your family here," J.C. continued. Lillian's short-term memory was nearly nonexistent, but she remembered quite a bit from the past.

"My Maddie, yes."

J.C. glanced in Maddie's direction to include her in the conversation. "Just one child?"

"One perfect daughter," Lillian declared proudly.

Maddie felt her cheeks warming and shrugged an embarrassed apology to the doctor.

He grinned. "And why mess with perfection?"

"That's how we always felt," Lillian agreed with a vigorous nod as she turned to stare at her daughter.

J.C. mimicked her action.

Maddie immediately wished she'd remembered to wear lipstick. And what had she been thinking when she'd chosen this rumpled blouse and skirt? *That her mother had let the bath water run unchecked until it overflowed. And Maddie had been zooming on full speed to get the mess cleaned up so that they could get ready for the appointment. Their small home had only one bathroom and Lillian could have easily slipped on the tile floor.*

Self-consciously, Maddie smoothed her full cotton skirt, remembering she hadn't done a thing with her hair. In fact, she'd pulled it back in a messy ponytail. Just add the braces she'd once worn and she would look as geeky as she had in high school. Trying not to flush more, Maddie smiled feebly beneath their inspection.

"Maddie should have her own tea shop," Lillian continued.

"Oh, yes?"

Maddie squirmed. "Just an old dream."

"Nothing of the kind," Lillian declared. "She should set up right on Main Street, smack dab in the middle of town."

"Let me know when you're ready," J.C. gazed at Maddie. "I happen to have a building...well, actually it belongs to my young niece. And it desperately needs a tenant. Be a great place for a tea shop." Turning back to Lillian, he extended his hand. "Mrs. Carter, I've enjoyed our visit and I'm looking forward to seeing you more often."

"I should think you'd rather visit with my beautiful daughter," Lillian guilelessly replied.

Lord, a hole, please. Underneath this chair, just big enough for me to disappear.

"I'll see you both on your next visit," J.C. replied without missing a beat.

Rumpled, crumpled and thoroughly embarrassed, Maddie rose, ready to end their consultation.

But the doctor wasn't. This time he spoke directly

to her. "My nurse will set up the tests." He held out a paper. "Just give this to her." He scribbled on a second sheet of paper. "And I want to adjust your mother's medications."

"Thank…" Maddie cleared the embarrassing croaking in her voice. "Thank you."

"My pleasure."

She sincerely doubted that, but smiled. "Mom, should we go home? Have that cup of tea?"

"Maddie makes the best tea in the world," Lillian announced, this time her voice not as strong. She weakened quickly these days.

J.C. opened the exam room door, allowing them to precede him. Maddie wasn't sure how she knew, but she was almost certain that J.C. continued watching as they left. She had a wild impulse to look back, to see. But there wasn't any point. Her social life had ended when her mother's dementia had begun. And mooning over a handsome doctor would only make her long for what wasn't in her destiny.

"Maddie?"

"Yes, Mom."

"I have a yen for some tea. What do you think?"

That she needed to put longings out of her head. This was her reality. "Sounds good."

Lillian patted her hand, having completely forgotten Maddie's words only minutes before. J.C. wouldn't be part of her own future, but Maddie was fiercely glad he was in her mother's. At the rate she was deteriorating, otherwise, Lillian might lose her grip on even the distant past.

Chilled by the possibility, Maddie gently squeezed her mother's delicate fingers. They were the last remaining members of their family. It didn't bear thinking how dreadful it would be should that tiny number be halved.

J.C. stared after his departing patient. Well, her daughter, actually. Not that he'd forgotten a detail about Lillian.

Or Maddie. Refreshing. The one word summed her up completely. From the sprinkle of freckles on her smooth skin to the strawberry-blond wisps of hair that escaped from her bouncy ponytail. His gut reaction to her had come out of nowhere. That door had been closed since his ex-wife's betrayal. Now with everything else in his life...

The intercom in his office buzzed. "Dr. M?"

"I'm here, Didi."

"School's on the phone."

He sighed. His nine-year-old niece, Chrissy, wasn't adjusting well after the deaths of her parents. It had been a blow out of the blue. His sister, Fran, and brother-in-law, Jay, had been asleep when carbon monoxide had leaked out of the furnace. Chrissy, their only child, had been at a friend's pajama party for the night.

"Dr. M?" Didi called again.

"Yeah, I'll get it." Reluctantly he picked up the phone.

"Doctor Mueller?"

J.C. readily recognized the principal's voice. They'd spoken often since the tragedy. "Yes, David?"

"You need to pick up Chrissy."

Frowning, he checked his watch. It was only eleven in the morning. "Now?"

"There's been another... incident."

Chrissy, once a model child and student, had been acting out. "Surely she doesn't need to come home this early in the day."

"Afraid so, J.C." The principal dropped the formalities. "She started a fight with two other girls. One is in tears, the other had to go home because we couldn't calm her down. J.C., you're going to have to figure out how to get Chrissy back under control."

J.C. rubbed his forehead, feeling the onset of now near-constant pain. He'd easily diagnosed himself. Stress-induced migraines. Losing his only sibling had been a devastating blow. He and his older sister had always been close. She'd been the one always looking out for him, the one who had comforted him when they'd lost first their father, then not long afterward their mother. And she'd kept him propped up during his divorce. Without her...

Fran had been his pillar. Illogically, he wanted

to speak to her, so she could tell him how to deal with Chrissy.

Opening the day's schedule on his laptop, J.C. saw that he could steal an hour by switching one consultation. After asking Didi to make the arrangements, he drove quickly to the nearby school.

Chrissy sat in one of the chairs in the office, her arms crossed, her expression mute. But her posture and body spoke for her. Sulky. From the top of her head to the tips of her crossed feet.

She didn't meet his gaze while he talked with the secretary and checked Chrissy out of school. But once in the hallway, her footsteps dragged.

J.C. couldn't be mad. Under her rebellious expression was a hurt little girl overwhelmed by pain and loss. He placed one hand on her shoulder as they walked side-by-side, both silent as they approached the car.

Chrissy pulled off her backpack and flung it on the floor. Along with the clicking of seat belts being fastened in place, they were the only sounds until he turned the key in the ignition. J.C. drove out of the school parking lot before he spoke. "You'll have to spend the afternoon at the office."

Chrissy stared out the window. "I'm old enough to stay by myself."

Thinking how vulnerable she was, he kept his tone light. "I'm not sure *I'm* old enough to stay on my own. At any rate, you'll have more space to spread out your books in Mrs. Cook's office."

Chrissy snorted.

J.C. glanced over at his niece. She still stared out the window. The only time she reacted positively was when they passed Wagner Hill House, the building on Main Street that had contained her father's business. It had sat undisturbed since Jay's death.

Thinking it might help Chrissy, J.C. decided to drive by his sister's house. Although he kept putting it off, he needed to sort through the house, make it livable again. Maybe Chrissy would settle down if she could live in her home again. He didn't mind giving up his tiny apartment; it was just a place to sleep really.

Turning on Magnolia Avenue, he saw Chrissy straighten up.

Pleased she was finally showing interest in something, he pulled into the driveway.

As soon as he turned off the vehicle, Chrissy began shrieking.

"No! I won't go in! No! No!" Sobs erupted and tears flooded her cheeks. "You can't make me!"

Horrified, J.C. tried to calm her. "What is it, Chrissy?"

"The house killed them!" She blurted out between staggered sobs.

Her distress was so intense J.C. didn't try to reason with her. Instead, he quickly backed out of the driveway, then sped from the neighborhood. Once past the familiar streets, he pulled into a space in front of the park. Unhooking his own seat belt and then Chrissy's, he gently guided her from the car to a bench beneath a large oak.

Still shaking from the remaining gulps of tears, she allowed him to drape an arm over her shoulders. When she was tiny, he would have popped her in his lap, pulled a dozen silly faces and made her giggle. He felt completely ill-equipped to comfort her now.

Patting her arm, he waited until the last of her hiccupping gulps trailed to an end. "I'm sorry, Chrissy. I wouldn't have gone to the house if I'd known it would upset you." He paused. "I was hoping it would make you feel better."

She shook her head so hard that her light brown hair flew unchecked from side to side. "I never, ever want to go there again."

"After some time—"

"Never!" she exclaimed. Her lips wobbled and a few new tears mixed with the wash of others on her cheeks.

J.C. patted her knee. "I thought you might like to live there again, get out of my scruffy apartment."

"No!" she cried again, burying her face against his shoulder. "I can't!"

J.C. imagined he could hear the child's heart actually breaking. "Then you won't." He would have the contents packed for storage, then rent out the house in case she changed her mind later. "And if it starts bothering you, we won't go by the print building, either."

Chrissy pulled back a bit so she could look at him. "It's not the same."

"No?"

"Daddy's work didn't hurt them. It was the house."

Logic wasn't a factor. Just the raw feelings of a wounded child.

"Okay, then."

"We could move in there," she suggested hopefully. "To Daddy's work."

The first floor of the building had been occupied by the business. And there were two apartments above it. Jay's parents had lived in one until they passed away.

"No one's lived in those apartments for a while," he explained. More important, they wouldn't have any immediate neighbors. Even though his bachelor apartment was small, at least in his complex, Chrissy was surrounded by people. He didn't like the idea of her being alone in a big building on Main Street when he had to make night calls at the hospital. A few proprietors lived above their businesses, but not in the building next to them. And the Wagner Hill House was on a corner next to a side street that bisected Main, so there wasn't a second adjoining neighbor.

"We could fix up the apartment," Chrissy beseeched, kicking her feet back, dragging them through the grass. "And live on top of Daddy's print shop." The apartment was above the business on the second floor, but he knew what she meant.

Blair, a nurse who worked at the hospital, lived in his apartment complex and so far J.C. had asked her to listen for Chrissy when he had to leave her. But it wasn't a comfortable situation. He worried the entire time he was away. What if Chrissy woke up and was scared? What if there was a fire? The possibilities were endless. But he couldn't hire live-in help to share their small space. As it was, he was camping out on the sofa so Chrissy could have the only bedroom.

And babysitters weren't pleased to be phoned in the middle of the night. The few who had reluctantly responded once didn't respond again. Not that J.C. blamed them. Who wanted to get up at two or three in the morning to babysit, not knowing if they would have to stay an hour or the rest of the night? What they really needed was sort of a combination housekeeper and nanny who lived in. But Chrissy had run off every single one he had hired, resenting anyone she thought was trying to take her mother's place.

"I'm afraid we can't live in the Main Street building."

Chrissy sniffled. "Then are we going to stay in your apartment?"

J.C. glanced up at the cloudless sky. Rosewood's tranquility had always been a peaceful balm. But now he wasn't certain there could be peace anywhere. *Lord, we need your help. Chrissy deserves more than just me. Please help us find the answer.*

Sighing, Chrissy leaned her head against his arm, her soft weight slumping dispiritedly.

Please, Lord.

Chapter Two

Maddie pulled one of her numerous tins of tea from a shelf in the pantry. "Sure you don't have a preference?"

Samantha Conway, Maddie's best friend and one-time neighbor, shrugged. "Surprise me. How many blends have you made now? One hundred?"

"Afraid not." She placed the tin on the table. "I have ideas for twice that many and space for less than thirty." Collecting two porcelain cups and saucers she added them to the table.

"So, did your mother like J.C.?" Samantha questioned.

"You were right all along. I should have taken her sooner," Maddie admitted. Samantha had raved about J.C. ever since he successfully treated her paralysis. Now Samantha walked with only a cane. She had been urging Maddie to see him about Lillian's worsening symptoms long before their G.P. had made his recommendation. "He's already ordered new tests and altered her medications." Swallowing, Maddie remembered the touch of his hand when he gave her the slip of paper.

"Earth to Maddie," Samantha repeated. "Something on your mind?"

"Of course not." Trying to sideline her friend's curiosity, Maddie got up and retrieved the electric kettle. Pouring water into their cups, she set the kettle on a trivet.

"Um, I hate to complain," Samantha began, "but we don't have any tea in our cups."

Maddie shook her face in tiny rapid nods. "Where's my head?" Because she used loose tea leaves to make her own private blends, she also used individual cup strainers. She put one on each of their cups, then added a scoop of tea leaves. She'd made so much tea over the years that she didn't need to measure the amount.

Samantha fiddled with her cup. "You sure you're okay?"

"Why?"

"For one, the strainer's sitting over the water, so I'm guessing the tea leaves aren't actually wet and…" She looked intensely at her friend. "The water's cold."

"Cold?" Maddie frowned. "It can't be cold. I just got it from the kettle." Poking her finger in the cup, she expected a hot jolt. *Cold water and limp tea leaves. Great.* "I hope the kettle's not broken." But as she checked the adjustments and made sure the base was plugged in, Maddie couldn't remember if she'd actually pushed the On button.

"Okay, give," Samantha urged. "You forgot to put the *tea* in the tea? And then you forgot to turn on the kettle? That's not like you."

"I suppose it's been a stressful day." She recounted the mishap with the morning bath water, how flustered she'd been trying to get them to the appointment on time. "I felt like my accelerator was stuck," she explained. "Filling in all the forms like a maniac as fast as I could, trying not to cause more delay…"

Samantha leaned back, studying her. "Just the letdown after an adrenaline rush?"

"I suppose so."

"Funny. You have at least one crisis a week with Lillian, but you've never offered me a cold cup of water that hasn't even swum close to a tea leaf."

Maddie waved her hands. "Then I'm having an off day."

"You haven't told me what you thought of J.C."

Maddie willed the sudden warmth in her neck to stay there and not redden her face. "He was fine."

"Fine?"

"Nice, then."

"Nice?"

"At this rate we'll be chattering away all day," Maddie observed with a wry twist of her lips. "I told you that Dr. Mueller ordered several tests and he's altered Mom's medications. He thinks one may be sedating her instead of treating the dementia."

"Um." Samantha studied her intently. "And that's all?"

Maddie fiddled with the worn tablecloth. "It was just our first visit."

"You plan on going back?"

"Of course!" Maddie replied in an instant. Inwardly grimacing, she slowed her words. "Providing Mom does better on the new medications." The kettle whistled. Relieved, she rose to get the hot water, using the excuse to try and straighten her muddled thoughts. Taking a deep breath, she returned, carefully pouring the steaming water into their cups. "I should have noticed that there wasn't any steam before. So, would you like some cookies with your tea?"

Looking truly concerned, Samantha drew her brows together, then pointed to a plate of lemon bars. "I brought these, remember?"

"Of course!" She clapped both hands over her reddening cheeks, then sank into her chair. "Not. I've been in a fluster since I got home."

Worry colored Samantha's eyes. "Is there something about Lillian's condition you haven't told me?"

Maddie shook her head. Thank heavens her mother was enjoying her regular afternoon nap and couldn't overhear. Lifting one shoulder in a half shrug, Maddie stared down at the delicate pink roses edging her saucer. "It's so stupid, it's not worth repeating really."

Samantha leaned forward. "If it's got you this upset—"

"I wouldn't exactly call it upsetting. Well, maybe. Depends on what you—"

Rapping the table with her knuckles, Samantha cut off her words. "Spill it."

"I thought… I think Dr. Mueller is…well, attractive."

"Downright handsome to be precise. How can this be a surprise? Surely you've seen him around town?"

"Mom's doctor is in an old building downtown, not in the hospital where Dr. Mueller works. Thankfully, we haven't had to be at the hospital much."

"Still…" Samantha stopped abruptly. "Sorry. Of course I know you don't get out enough. I just thought that somehow…" She brightened. "But you do like him?"

"He's nice."

"Don't start that again. And you can call him J.C." Samantha wriggled her eyebrows. "He's single, you know. Well, divorced actually."

"Divorced?"

"I don't know the details, but I understand it was bad."

Maddie wondered why any woman would let him go. Silly, she didn't know a thing about him. Other than that smile, those eyes… Abruptly, she shook her head. "Honestly, Sam, you're the last person I expected to matchmake. We're seeing him so he can help Mom, not so I can develop a crush." The word was barely out of her mouth when Maddie wished she could draw it back.

Samantha blinked.

"Bad choice of words," Maddie tried to explain.

"Accurate is more like it." She smiled more gently. "Hit that hard, did it?"

Her embarrassment waning, Maddie plopped her chin on one outstretched hand. "Stupid, huh? I'm old enough to know better."

"You're not *that* old," Samantha objected. "Besides, I don't believe in an age limit on falling in love."

"Whoa!" Maddie protested. "Who said anything about love?"

Samantha grinned. "Puppy love?"

"I had my chance. I picked taking care of Mom instead. It's what I want." Maddie wasn't only loyal, she couldn't imagine shuttling her mother away because it was more convenient.

"It doesn't have to be a choice." Samantha patted Maddie's hand. "Lillian wants you to be happy."

"And a man deserves a woman who can devote herself to him and the family they create. I'm not that woman." Although she'd never regretted her choice, Maddie sometimes dreamed of a life with a loving husband and children of her own. It wasn't her destiny, but the fantasy was harmless.

"You just haven't met the right man yet," Samantha insisted in a gentle, yet confident, tone.

"Forgetting Owen, aren't you?" Maddie's high school, then college sweetheart, they'd been engaged when her mother had suffered the first of many strokes. Lillian had only been in her forties at the time, young for the onset of the neurological nightmare that had stolen her short-term memory.

Samantha's expression was steady. "He's a rat. What kind of man asks you to choose between him and your mother? He knew what was going on, how painful it was for you to give up everything."

Maddie tried to interrupt. "But—"

"But nothing. I know you'd make the same choice again, but asking you to put her in a nursing home..." Samantha shook her head angrily. "And it's not as though he was new to your life, didn't know your history."

Stroking the silken smoothness of the porcelain cup, Maddie remembered Owen's unyielding stance. "I did think he might understand. We were going together when my dad passed away."

"He also knew you didn't have any relatives to share the load." Samantha's fierce loyalty didn't waver. "Total rat."

Maddie reluctantly smiled. "That's a little extreme, don't you think?"

"Nope." Loyal to the end, Samantha didn't give an inch. "And J.C.'s about as different from Owen as a *rat* is to a cat."

"I wouldn't have thought it until you came back to Rosewood, but you're a romantic, Sam. Just because you and Bret got back together after nearly a decade—"

"That was fate," Samantha insisted. "And real, genuine, honest love. It wasn't a reunion, it was a new start."

"I imagine Owen's got his hands full with his business." His family had money, and Owen had stepped into the enviable position of entrepreneur with none of the struggle most young business owners faced.

"Hmm. And, yes, I know, Bret's running his family business, but it wasn't stuffed with cash."

In fact, it was almost failing when Bret took the helm. "No comparison, Sam. I agree. When we were younger I didn't think Owen was that affected by having…okay, everything. He just seemed to take it in stride. But when he got older…" He wasn't the boy she'd fallen in love with.

"Hey, I'm sorry." Samantha's voice changed to one of concern. "I didn't mean to stir all that up. I guess I just thought…well, J.C.'s such a great guy, and you're my best friend…" She smiled encouragingly. "I still think your life's going to change because of him—he's going to help Lillian and that'll help you."

"It's not as though I don't daydream myself. And you're right. If he can help Mom…" Maddie smiled.

"That's all I ask." *Because her other dreams were just flotsam in the ether. And as likely to materialize.*

True to his word, J.C. began Lillian's tests with a noninvasive CT scan. Officially called computed tomography, it could detect a blood clot or intracranial bleeding in patients with a stroke. And the scan aided in differentiating the area of the brain affected by the disorder.

J.C. had prescribed a light sedative so that Lillian could lie still. Forgetting where she was, otherwise Lillian might have tried to move, skewing the test results.

The test took only about thirty minutes, but Maddie paced in the waiting room. She didn't want her mother to wake up disoriented and scared. The technician had assured her that he would watch out for Lillian during the scan, but Maddie couldn't stop worrying.

"She's all right," J.C. announced quietly from behind her.

Maddie whirled around. The carpeted waiting area had camouflaged the sound of his footsteps.

Dressed in scrubs, he acted as though it was normal for him to deliver the news, rather than the technician.

Maddie began to shake, fearing the worst. "Was there a problem?"

He stepped closer, his eyes flickering over her trembling limbs. "None whatsoever. I didn't mean to alarm you. I just got out of surgery, thought I'd pop in and check on your mother."

Relieved, Maddie exhaled, her chest still rising with the effort to breathe normally.

J.C. took her arm, guiding her to a chair. "You're going to have to take it easy."

Perched on the edge of the chair, she stared up at him.

"CT scan's about the mildest procedure your mother's going to have. You'll sap your energy if you get this upset about every test."

Suddenly Maddie could breathe. And stand. Nearly nose to nose with him. "I know you're an excellent doctor. Samantha Conway is proof of that. But don't presume to tell me how to react. I've been caring for my mother for years. I know she gets confused and scared..." Maddie's trembling increased. "And I won't let anyone make that worse."

"Good."

Maddie blinked.

"A dedicated caregiver is the best medicine any patient can have." J.C.'s tone remained mild. His gold-flecked brown eyes were more elusive. "I'll call you when I have the results. Should be about two days." With a nod, he left.

Maddie wasn't certain what to think. Plopping the palm of her hand against her forehead, she wished she could travel back in time a few minutes. This doctor was a road of hope for her mother and she'd just insulted him. Refusing to consider that her defensive reaction could have anything to do with her attraction to him, she bit down on her thumbnail.

Catching sight of the technician, she tried to shove the thoughts away and decided it would be easier to tame an infuriated horde of wasps.

J.C. strode down the familiar corridors toward his office. The sandy-beige walls were lined with portraits of the hospital's founders and patrons. But he wasn't looking at any of them. He wanted to kick something, preferably himself. Maddie Carter had been on his mind since the day they'd met. He'd sensed an empathetic soul. One who could understand what he was going through.

A tall, slim man in a white coat plopped himself in J.C.'s path. "Someone put cactus needles in your scrubs?"

J.C. immediately recognized the voice. "Adam."

His colleague and friend Adam Winston tugged at the stethoscope looped around his neck. "I don't normally drive into tornados, but from the look on your face, I think you might need some help getting out of the storm."

"Just a mild gale." J.C. exhaled. "Put too much thought into a nitwit notion."

"Why don't I believe that?"

"Don't you have rounds?"

Adam shrugged. "Not for another hour." Amiable, persistent, often brilliant, Adam wasn't going anywhere without an answer.

J.C. summarized his two meetings with Maddie. "That's it," he concluded.

Adam's knowing look was both confusing and annoying. "Uh-huh."

"Don't try to make something out of this."

Whistling, Adam winked, then briefly shook his head. "I don't need to. You've got that covered."

J.C. clenched his teeth. Realizing he had, he made himself relax.

"Hasn't it occurred to you that this woman's under just as much strain as you are?" Adam continued. "When she saw you instead of the tech, she probably thought her mother had suffered another stroke. Wouldn't be the first time a test triggered one."

"I'm sure she's stressed."

"Are you? Have you checked out the situation? Does anyone help care for the mother? Or is she on her own?"

Remembering that Lillian had said Maddie was an only child, J.C. didn't reply.

"If she's the full-time live-in caregiver, you know she could be ready to crack." Adam twirled the end of his stethoscope.

J.C. hadn't asked about the details of Lillian Carter's care. Had he done what he'd despised in others? Judged without knowing the facts? Worse even, judging at all?

Chapter Three

J.C. pulled into the semicircle driveway at the front of the Rosewood Community Church school. He was late. Again. Didi had picked up Chrissy a few times for him, but she was busy. Besides, he couldn't expect his employees and friends to sacrifice any more than they already had.

The school was nearly deserted. Only the teachers' cars remained in the parking lot and a few kids were kicking a ball on the playground. Chrissy sat on the steps, clutching her backpack, looking lost.

Poor kid. First she felt deserted when her parents died; now she felt just as abandoned by him. Turning off the car, he got out to meet her halfway. Her face was more than sullen; fear and vulnerability were just as apparent.

"Chrissy, I'm sorry. No excuses. I'm late."

Although she tried to control it, her lips wobbled. "I know."

"How about a big chocolate shake at the drugstore?" The old-fashioned marble fountain was one of Chrissy's favorite places.

"Uh-uh," she replied, shaking her head.

J.C. would have reached for the child's backpack so he could carry it to the car, but she still clutched it like a lifeline. She'd had the backpack with her at the pajama party, untouched by the poisonous carbon monoxide. Untouched by what had changed her life forever.

J.C. wished he could think of something to distract her, to ease the pain from her face. But fun hadn't been on the agenda for quite a while now.

Chrissy settled in her seat, scooting forward suddenly, pulling up a bag that was wedged beneath her. "What's this?"

"Some trial medications for a new patient. I've been meaning to drop them off…" But every time he thought about it, he pictured Maddie's anger.

"Why don't we go now?"

He stared at his niece. "You *want* to go?"

She shrugged. "Nothing else to do."

Except a mountain of dictation, articles, more work than he wanted to think about. "Right." But the stop would distract Chrissy. "Nothing else to do."

The Carter home wasn't far. J.C. had copied their address on the sample bag. Located in one of Rosewood's oldest neighborhoods, the house was an unimposing Victorian. Neither grand nor tiny, it spoke of the families that had inhabited it over the generations. The yard and flower beds were tidy, the porch and driveway well swept. But he noticed the aging roof and the peeling paint on the second-story fascia and gables.

An aged but inviting swing flanked two well-worn rocking chairs on the wide porch. It was quiet as they climbed the steps, then knocked on the outer screen door.

Within just a few moments the door swung open. Taken aback, Maddie stared at him, then collected her voice. "Dr. Mueller, I wasn't expecting you." Her gaze shifted to include Chrissy. "Hello."

Chrissy ducked just a fraction behind him. J.C. put a reassuring hand on her shoulder. "This is my niece, Chrissy."

"Good to meet you, Chrissy." Maddie pushed the screen door back. "Come in. I just put the kettle on."

Chrissy looked up at him in question.

J.C. patted her back. "Actually, we just stopped to drop off samples of a new medication for your mother."

"Do you have time for tea?" Maddie asked, not a bit of the anger he remembered anywhere in sight.

He glanced down at his niece. She didn't look averse to the idea. "I guess so. Thanks."

"Mom's in the living room," Maddie explained, leading the way from the small entry hall. She glanced at Chrissy. "In a house this old, they used to call the front room a parlor, but ours isn't the elegant sort."

Looking intrigued, Chrissy listened quietly.

"Mom? Dr. Mueller stopped by to have tea."

Lillian sat in a faded green rocker recliner. Seeing her guests, she brightened. "I love meeting new people!"

"This is Dr. Mueller's niece, Chrissy," Maddie began.

Lillian clapped her hands together. "Oh, my! You look an awful lot like my Maddie when she was your age." She patted the chair next to hers. "Come. Sit."

Chrissy's normal reluctance dimmed and she crossed the room. "I thought you knew my uncle James."

Lillian smiled. "Perhaps I do. You'll have to tell me all about him."

Chrissy looked at him, then turned back to Lillian. "He's a doctor. And he's *real* busy."

J.C. flinched.

"I imagine you stay busy with school." Lillian's gaze landed on the ever-present backpack. "Just like my Maddie, always did her homework straightaway."

Chrissy stroked the pink bag and halfheartedly shrugged. "Sometimes."

Lillian's eyes glinted with mischief. "Sometimes we baked cookies first or built a playhouse."

"You built a playhouse?" Chrissy asked in wonder as Lillian dug into the purse that was always at her side.

Lillian produced a roll of Life Savers and offered them to Chrissy. "Sure did. My father thought a girl should know how to use a hammer and a saw. He liked to make things with his hands, so he taught me in his workshop."

Chrissy swallowed. "My dad did, too."

Lillian patted her knee. "Sounds like we had wonderful fathers."

Strange. It was as though somehow Lillian sensed Chrissy's father was gone, as well.

J.C. heard a whistle from the other side of the house. No doubt the teakettle. Considering, he watched his niece, saw that her attention was entirely focused on Lillian. Pivoting, he followed the sound of the fading whistle to the kitchen. A carpet runner covered the oak floor in the long hall; it also muffled the sound of his footsteps.

He paused beneath the arched opening to the kitchen. Maddie was scurrying around the room, pushing strawberry-blond hair off her forehead with one hand, reaching for a tray with the other. Seeing that it was perched on one of the higher shelves, he quickened his pace. "Let me get that for you."

Whirling around at the sound of his voice, she looked completely, totally, utterly flustered.

"Guess I need to stop doing that. Coming up from behind, surprising you."

Her throat worked and her blue-gray eyes looked chastened. "I feel terrible about how I reacted the other day. It's just that Mom's gotten so fragile, and…" Moisture gathered in her eyes and she quickly wiped it away. "I'm so afraid that the next stroke…" Again her throat worked, but she pushed past the emotion. "I know she needs these tests—"

J.C. lightly clasped her arm. "Being a caregiver is the most stressful job I can imagine. Do you have enough help?"

"Help?" Maddie nodded. "Samantha relieves me so that I have some extra time when I run errands, but she has her own family to take care of. Neighbors and people from church sit with Mom, too, when they can."

He'd reread the file and knew that Lillian was widowed. With no siblings, did that mean that Maddie was the sole caregiver? "It's important that you have time for yourself."

She laughed, a mirthless sound. "Hmm."

Spotting the cups on the table, he took her elbow, guiding her to the table. "Let's sit for a few minutes."

"But your niece—"

"Is taken by your mother. Best Chrissy's acted in a while. Tea smells good."

Distracted, Maddie glanced at the tabletop. "It's probably the vanilla you're smelling."

J.C. sat in the chair next to hers. "Who else helps you take care of Lillian?"

"Just me."

J.C. knew that endless caregiving could suck the life from a person. And Lillian had required home care for nearly a decade. "Have you lost some of your relief help?"

"Never had any." Picking up the sugar, she offered it to him.

"But when do you have time for yourself?"

She lifted the porcelain strainers from their cups. "I don't think of it like that. This is my life, my choice. It's hard for other people to understand."

"What about before Lillian's strokes? You must have had plans."

An indecipherable emotion flashed in her now bluish eyes and then disappeared. Had her eyes changed color? Or was it a trick of the light?

"That's the thing about the future," Maddie replied calmly. "It can always change. So far, mine has."

Since J.C. had witnessed that she wasn't always a serene earth muffin, he sipped his tea, wondering exactly who the real Maddie was. "This is unusual. Don't think I've ever tasted anything quite like it."

"The tea's my own blend," she explained.

"How did you come to make your own tea recipe?"

She chuckled, some of her weariness disappearing. "Not just one recipe. I blend all sorts of teas."

"Same question, then. How did you start making your own tea?"

"I've always been fascinated by spices. I can remember my grandfather telling me about the original spice routes from Asia and I could imagine all the smells, the excitement of the markets. So my mother let me collect spices and we'd make up recipes to use them in. Then one day I decided to add some fresh nutmeg to my tea." Her cheeks flushed as her enthusiasm grew. "Mom always made drinking tea an event—using the good cups, all the accessories. Anyway, Mom bought every kind of loose tea leaf she could find so I could experiment. For a time our kitchen looked like a cross between an English farmhouse and a laboratory. After college I planned to open a shop where I could sell all my blends." She leaned forward, her eyes dreamy. "And I'd serve fresh, hot tea on round bistro tables covered with white linen tablecloths. Oh, and little pastries, maybe sandwiches. Make it a place people want to linger…to come back to."

"The tea shop your mother said should be *smack dab in the middle of Main Street?*"

"Oh, yes."

"Did you ever get a shop set up?"

Maddie shook her head. "I was investigating small business loans when Mom had her first stroke, the major one. Luckily, I'd graduated from U.T. by then."

"Have you considered starting the business? Using part of the profits to hire someone to stay with your mother while you're working?"

"Our funds aren't that extensive. I took enough

business classes to know I'd have to factor in at least a year of loss before we'd show any profit. Or just staying even. Doesn't leave anything for caregiver salaries. Besides, Mom's happy with me."

"Don't forget I've got a building that needs a tenant if you change your mind. Plenty of room for a shop and tearoom." He swallowed more of his tea. "What about the senior center activities we talked about? That would fill several hours a day."

Maddie's smile dimmed. "As the first step toward a nursing home?"

"Nothing of the kind. If Lillian responds to her new medication, she could well enjoy spending time with people her own age."

"Her friends have been loyal," Maddie objected. "People stop by fairly often to visit her."

J.C. studied the obstinate set of her jaw. "But not to visit with you?"

Maddie looked down, fiddling with the dish towel still in her lap. "People my age have young families of their own to take care of."

A situation he knew only too well.

"It's difficult for someone who's never been in this position to understand," Maddie continued. "I'm sure you're busy with your work… and it probably consumes most of your time, but I can't walk away from my mother. It's not some martyr complex. It's my *choice*."

"And sometimes there isn't a choice."

Maddie scrunched her eyes in concentration.

"Your niece? Chrissy? You said something about how she was behaving. Is there a problem?"

J.C. explained how he'd come to be his niece's guardian. "I don't blame her for acting out. She's lost everyone she loves."

Unexpectedly, Maddie covered his hand with hers. "Not quite everyone."

He stared at her long, slender fingers.

"Dr. Mueller? J.C.?"

"Sorry." He pulled his gaze back to hers. "Chrissy's been fighting with some of the girls at school, her grades are slipping." And she was miserable.

"What about your babysitter? Do they get on well?"

"We've been through a parade of sitters and housekeepers. Can't keep one."

Concern etched Maddie's face. "Can I help? She could spend afternoons with us. Does she go to the community church school? We're in easy walking distance."

"Don't have enough on your plate?" J.C. was dumbfounded. Maddie claimed she wasn't a martyr, but…

"It's what we do."

He felt as blank as he must have looked.

"You know, here in Rosewood. She's a child who needs any help we can give her."

It was how J.C. had been raised, too. "Maybe from people who have the time. You're exhausted now. I'm not going to add to that burden."

The fire in her now stormy-gray eyes was one he remembered. "It's not a burden. I realize my situation isn't for everyone, but it works for me. And I have enough energy to spare some for Chrissy."

She was pretty remarkable, J.C. decided. Even more remarkable—she didn't seem to realize it.

Chapter Four

J.C. stood in front of his sister's closet in her far-too-quiet home. Fran's things were just as she'd left them. Not perfectly in order; she was always in too much of a hurry to fuss over details she had considered unimportant. No, she'd lavished her time on her family, especially Chrissy.

A cheery yellow scarf dangled over an ivory jacket, looking for all the world as though Fran had just hung it up. Anyone searching through the rooms would never conclude it had been a scene of death. Instead, it looked as though Fran, Jay and Chrissy could walk in any moment, pick up their lives.

Fran would be laughing, teasing Chrissy and Jay in turn, turning her hand at a dozen projects, baking J.C.'s favorite apple crumble, inviting friends over.

There hadn't been an awful lot of time to ask why. Why had they perished? Especially when each had so much to give. Caught up in trying to care for Chrissy, the questions had been shelved.

J.C. was on borrowed time even now. He had thought he could make some sort of inventory of the house so that he could set things in motion, have the important contents stored, the house rented. But he couldn't bring himself to even reach inside the closet.

Other people survived loss. As a doctor, he'd seen his share and then some. But how did they take that first step, put the gears in motion? Fran had managed when their parents passed away. She had thoughtfully sorted out mementos for each of them, things she had accurately predicted he would cherish. Now, he needed to do the same for Chrissy.

His friend Adam suggested hiring an estate service, one that could view everything with an eye to its current or future value. To J.C., the process sounded like an autopsy. Backing away from the closet, he tore out of the room. Striding quickly, he passed through the living room, then bolted outside. Breathing heavily, he sank into the glider on the porch, loosening his tie.

The breeze was lighter than a bag of feathers, but he drew in big gulps of air. He'd never been claustrophobic, but he felt as though he'd just been locked in an airless pit. He pictured Chrissy's stricken face. Maybe it wasn't so illogical that she wouldn't step foot in the house.

Lifting his head, he leaned back, his gaze drifting over the peaceful lane. School was in session, so no kids played in the yards or rode their bicycles in the street. A few houses down, Mrs. Morton was weeding her flower bed and a dog barked. Not that there was much to bark at. Extending his gaze, he spotted a woman pushing a wheelchair on the sidewalk across the street. The color of her hair stirred a note of recognition.

Maddie Carter? Shifting, he leaned forward, focusing on the pair. It was Maddie, pushing Lillian's wheelchair. Although Lillian could walk, she tired easily. Combined with the mental confusion, he understood why Maddie chose to use the chair.

They were within shouting distance when Maddie glanced across the street. Recognition dawned and she leaned down to say something to her mother. Walking a few feet farther, Maddie detoured off the sidewalk via a driveway and used the same method to reach the front of Fran's house.

Trying to tuck his emotions beneath a professional demeanor, J.C. walked down the steps.

Apparently he wasn't completely successful.

"What's wrong?" Maddie greeted him, her eyes filled with sudden concern. Today her eyes picked up some of the green of the grass, rendering them near-emerald.

J.C. straightened his tie, but couldn't bring himself to pull it into a knot. The strangled feeling from being in Fran's house hadn't dissipated. "This is my sister's house."

Understanding flooded Maddie's expression. "Are you here by yourself?"

J.C. nodded. "Chrissy won't come back."

"What can we do?"

He glanced at the wheelchair. "Your hands are full enough."

Maddie patted Lillian's shoulder in a soothing motion. "My mother always enjoys visiting new places." She met his gaze. Both knew most anywhere other than her own home was now a new place for Lillian.

The older woman smiled at him kindly. "Young man, you need a bracing cup of tea."

Apparently even his patient could see his distress. "I don't have the makings for tea."

"We do," Lillian replied, craning her head around and up toward Maddie. "Don't we?"

"Yes, but maybe Dr. Mueller would like to just sit on the porch."

"Well, now, I'd like that myself," Lillian replied.

Shedding his own worries, J.C. offered his arm. "Would you care to sit in the glider?"

She giggled, a young, fun sound. "I always have."

As he helped her rise from the wheelchair, J.C. imagined she'd had a fair share of male attention in her youth. In ways, he could see an advantage in having only partial memories. Hopefully the bad ones faded and only the good stayed.

Once Lillian was settled on the glider, he pulled two rattan chairs close, offering one to Maddie.

With the glider set in gentle motion, Lillian's eyelids fluttered near closing.

"What was it?" Speaking quietly, Maddie tilted her head toward the house. "Inside?"

J.C. thought of a dozen noncommittal answers. "Everything."

"It was hard after my dad died," Maddie sympathized. "You said Chrissy won't come back?"

"Completely freaked out when I tried," he replied in an equally quiet tone. "Said she never wants to come back, that the house killed her parents."

Maddie's forehead furrowed. "Were you thinking of moving in here, so Chrissy would have all her familiar things?"

"That and because we're two people living in a one-person tent. So to speak," he explained. "I have a small one-bedroom apartment and it's not good."

"And you're certain Chrissy won't change her mind?"

"Absolutely."

Maddie hesitated. "Are you going to sell the house?"

"Thought about renting it out in case Chrissy changes her mind in the future. But right now…I can't rent it with all of my sister's belongings still inside."

"That's what got to you," Maddie murmured. "There's still a sweater and bathrobe of my dad's in Mom's closet."

The dog down the street barked again. And Mrs. Morton crossed the street to talk to her neighbor.

J.C. barely knew Maddie. Funny to be having this conversation with her. But none of his friends could really empathize. Some had lost a parent, but no one had lost everyone. Certainly no one else had the crucial role of caring for the sole survivor.

Maddie swiped at her wayward hair. He liked the way it sprang back with a mind of its own. "Do you have anyone to help you go through your sister's belongings?"

He shrugged one shoulder. "No one else will know what's important."

"Not necessarily," she objected mildly. "Thinking of things in categories could help. You can decide if there's a special garment, like my dad's sweater, you want to save. If not, then it doesn't take a personal eye to empty closets. Same is pretty much true for the kitchen with the exception of heirloom pieces. Furniture can be sorted through, or just stored for now. Jewelry, papers, other keepsakes can be packed and labeled for when you feel it's time to decide about them."

J.C. sighed. "You make it sound reasonable—"

"It is if you'll accept help."

"It's not a job I can ask anyone to tackle."

"You didn't ask. I'm offering." With her back against the cloudy gray exterior of the house, Maddie's eyes had changed again. But this time the gray held no storm warnings. "Before you mention my mother, she'll come with me. I'm guessing there's a comfortable chair and a television. It'll be an outing for her that isn't tiring."

"For her, maybe not. But you—"

"I can't believe I look that fragile," Maddie declared. "To hear you talk, I'm so delicate it's a wonder I don't blow away in the breeze." She held out one hand as though testing the air. "Even in this breeze. You, of all people, should know how good it makes a person feel to help someone. I'd like to help. You're doing Mom a world of good. I can already see small improvements. Besides, you and Chrissy need to be able to move on. Once this house is rented to another family, it won't seem so scary anymore."

"A friend suggested hiring an estate service," he admitted.

"That might be taking it a tad too impersonal. Do you recall grilling me about who helps with Mom? Now, it's my turn. Who helps with Chrissy? Who can sort through the house? If that's you, will it be between appointments and surgeries?"

"And I thought I felt bad being *inside* the house."

She laughed, tipping her head back, allowing the laughter to gather and spill like a bright waterfall. "Touché."

Somehow, his dread had disappeared.

Maddie held out her hand, palm side up, her eyes still dancing. "I'll need a key."

* * *

"I'm a little nervous," Maddie admitted, fitting the key in the lock.

"You should be." Samantha rolled her eyes. "I still can't believe—"

"Other-may," Maddie resorted to pig Latin to remind her friend of Lillian's presence.

"Oh, now you remember."

"I never forgot." The key to Fran's house turned easily and Maddie pushed open the door. "Mom, you like getting out, don't you?"

Lillian smiled. "I like new places."

Samantha rolled her eyes again. "And it'll be new for a month of Sundays."

Maddie elbowed her friend. "I thought you liked J.C."

"I didn't expect you to take on organizing his life."

Maddie flinched. "Do you think he feels that way? And quit rolling your eyes before they fall out of your head."

"The only one here out of her head—"

Maddie grasped the handles of her mother's wheelchair and pushed her inside. "How about some TV, Mom? The cable's still on, so you can watch a movie or Animal Planet."

Lillian considered. "Have I seen Animal Planet before?"

She watched it every day. "I think so." Flipping through the channels, Maddie put the TV on an old movie her mother had seen dozens of times. Fortunately, it was new to her each and every time. Uncapping the thermos of tea she'd brought, Maddie poured some in a cup and placed it on the table next to Lillian.

She caught up to Samantha in the hallway, where she stood, leaning slightly on her cane as she studied family pictures grouped over a console table. "Seems hard to believe they just went to sleep and never woke up."

"I don't know J.C. well enough to say this, but I think he feels the same way."

"As though he might wake up one day and find out it was all just a bad dream." Samantha shook her head. "That's how I felt about Andy." Samantha's brother had died in a plane crash, ending his young life far too soon.

Maddie linked her arm with Sam's. "What we're doing, it's a good way to give back."

Sam's voice thickened. "Yeah." When she had returned to Rosewood paralyzed from a fall, she'd nearly burned down her parents' entire home. She succeeded in destroying the kitchen. But friends and neighbors had stepped up, rebuilding it, making it even better than before. And in the process, she had reconnected with her old love and now husband, Bret. Sam cleared her throat. "Where do you want to start?"

"Master bedroom, I think. J.C. insists on hiring someone to move the boxes once they're packed, so

I'd like to retrieve the jewelry for his safety deposit box. Then I thought of recording an inventory." She held up her cell phone. "I can shoot photos of the big pieces to J.C., let him decide what to keep."

They entered the carpeted master bedroom, feet sinking pleasantly into the deep pile. The four-poster bed looked as antique as the fireplace it flanked. In the curve of the bay window was a cozy reading area.

"Nice," Sam murmured.

Maddie walked to the open closet, seeing what J.C. had, instantly understanding why it had been so difficult. Although Maddie hadn't known Fran, remnants of her personality remained.

"What does he want to do with the clothes?"

"Donate them. But I thought we might find one outfit that we'd tuck away for Chrissy."

"Wonder if Fran kept her wedding dress," Samantha mused.

"Oh, Sam! That's perfect! You old softie, I said you'd turned into a romantic."

Samantha grinned. "Okay. So we're both hopeless."

The doorbell rang. A young man sent by J.C. to deliver packing boxes offered his help. Maddie showed him to the dining room where he could assemble the flat cartons.

"Efficient," Samantha commented, sitting on the bed, folding clothes. "You're right. Emptying this room first will make it easier for J.C. The longer we put off clearing Andy's room, the worse it was."

Maddie crossed the room to the dresser, then slid open the top drawer. A vintage leather jewelry box sat inside. "I'm guessing Fran inherited her mother's jewelry. Two generations of mementos for Chrissy."

"Poor kid. I can't imagine losing my parents now...but when you're nine years old?" Samantha smoothed the lines of the dress she was folding. "Still, I can't help worrying about you. Even though you always act chipper, I know the constant caregiving gets to you. And now this..."

Maddie turned to speak, but Sam cut her off.

"I know, I know. Helping people makes you feel better. But face it, even you have to admit this is a depressing chore."

The jewelry box still in her hands, Maddie stroked it absently. "If you could have seen his eyes..."

Samantha sighed. "It's my own fault. I just didn't expect you to wind up..." she waved her hands around "...here."

Maddie thought of J.C.'s face, the bleak expression, the unexpected spark of hope. Swallowing, she wished it hadn't meant so very much to her.

Chapter Five

Adam sat on the edge of J.C.'s desk, flipping through the messages on his cell phone.

"Your office must miss you," J.C. told him drily as he signed a stack of insurance forms.

"Let Didi come to work for me and I'll stay out of your way."

J.C. grunted. "Last I heard, she's still loyal."

"Yeah. You have the women hooked."

J.C. wagged his head in disbelief. "A whole harem."

"What about the patient's daughter? Maddie?"

Feeling an unwanted burst of protectiveness, J.C. looked up. "What about her?"

Adam flung out upturned hands. "Give."

J.C. fiddled with his pen for a moment. "She offered to close up Fran's house."

The joking demeanor faded. "Wow."

"That's what I thought. I was at the house, felt like I was going to lose it and Maddie stopped by."

"Out of the blue?"

"She was taking her mother out on a walk and spotted me on the porch. We talked about Fran's things. Maddie said it would be harder the longer I left it."

"What about the estate people?"

J.C. sighed. "I know you were trying to help, but it sounded so…cold. Maddie's going to take an inventory, get things packed for storage so I can rent out the house."

"Good plan. Then if Chrissy wants it later…"

"That's what we thought."

"We?"

"Lay off, Adam. Maddie's just trying to help because she's grateful that her mother's improving."

"Uh-huh."

"You need to get married, get off the romance radar."

"Because that worked out so well for you?"

J.C. winced. "There are downsides to having old friends. They know too much."

"Sorry. You know I get jittery about the marriage thing."

"Guess you haven't met the right woman." J.C. held up one hand before his friend could jump in with an obvious reminder. "And neither have I."

Adam raised his eyebrows. "Maybe you have, my friend."

J.C. frowned.

"Maddie sounds like someone worth getting to know."

"Ah, just what I need in my upside-down life."

Chuckling, Adam looked smug. "You said it."

A few weeks later, J.C. glanced around the near-empty rooms of his sister's house. "You're amazing!"

Surprisingly, Maddie blushed.

The quaint sign was charming, taking him aback even more than all she had accomplished.

"You sent a lot of help," she reminded him, not quite meeting his gaze as she fiddled with one of the few remaining cartons.

"Still…" He shifted, taking in how much had been accomplished, how his sister's belongings had all been tucked away.

"I did think of something else." Maddie finally lifted her eyes. Today they were as blue as her sapphire-colored blouse. "Even with another family living here, from the outside the house looks the same. If you had it painted in a new palette, one that doesn't even resemble the gray, it would seem very different."

J.C. hadn't even considered the exterior. "I don't know much about picking out colors."

Maddie smiled, causing the dimple in her cheek to flash. "That's the easy part."

Wanting to study her face, her soft-looking lips, he nodded. "Such as?"

She brushed a lock of hair from her forehead. "Um… yellow would be pretty. A daisy shade of yellow. White trim. Because the front door is mostly glass…" Her voice trailed off.

J.C. realized he was staring, not listening. "Sounds good."

She brightened. "I don't want you to think I'm meddling. I have this habit of over-organizing things, people, well, most everything."

Her dimple moved when she spoke, a punctuation mark to her smile. As he watched, it gradually disappeared. What had she just said?

Maddie's smile faded a bit.

And J.C. marshaled his thoughts. "You were saying?"

"That I meddle."

"Thank the Lord you do." She paled and he instantly realized she'd taken his words the wrong way. "Helping, not meddling. I'd never have guessed Fran's house could be packed up so… quickly."

"And the painting?" she prodded.

"Great idea." Her eyes were incredibly blue. "Maybe blue?"

"With the yellow? Or just a light shade of blue?"

"Definitely not light," he murmured, captivated by the depth of color in her eyes.

"Well, we could get some samples, look them over." Maddie twisted her hands.

J.C.'s gaze followed her action when he abruptly remembered the last time he'd been entranced by a pretty face and mesmerizing eyes. His ex-wife had been pretty, as well. On the outside. "You still haven't told me how much you'll take for doing all this."

Her eyes clouded and that enchanting dimple disappeared. "I did it to help you, not to make money."

"But…" He waved around, again stunned by the emptiness. While it was a relief to have the job done, the house no longer held the reminders of Fran's life. Facing Maddie again, he couldn't keep a sliver of bleakness out of his voice. "It was a big job."

Maddie's voice, too, was quiet. "For me it was Dad's fishing pole. Mom gave it to his best friend. Logically, I knew Dad was gone, that he wasn't coming back, but when his fishing pole was in the shed, leaning against the wall, it almost seemed like he'd stroll back in, whistling, ready to tie new flies."

She got it. Completely. "Yeah."

"When everything's done…if you do decide to change the look of the exterior, it might help Chrissy to see it's just a house."

His niece had been campaigning to live in the building on Main Street. "She'd kick and scream all the way here. And *I'm* not ready for that."

"Think about my offer."

He blanked, looking at her in question.

"To watch Chrissy in the afternoons."

"Still not enough to do?" he asked wryly.

"Actually, Chrissy kept Mom entertained the day

you visited. That means more time for me to get things done."

He was skeptical. "You forget, I *know* Chrissy. Much as I love her, right now she's acting like a pain."

"Understandably."

"It's easier to be understanding from a distance," he warned her, thinking of Chrissy's refusal to do any homework. He'd wrangled with her for more than an hour and had gotten nowhere.

Maddie laughed. "Isn't everything? Keep the offer in mind. I'm not going anywhere."

Sobered, he wondered. In his experience, that's exactly what women did.

The phone jangled loudly. J.C. bolted upright, reaching for the receiver before the noise could wake Chrissy. Momentarily forgetting he was sleeping on the couch, he overshot the mark and slammed his hand into a lamp that crashed to the floor. Grabbing the side table so that he wouldn't land on top of the broken glass, he smashed his toes into the unyielding wood base.

Muttering under his breath, he finally reached the phone. Bad car accident on the highway, possible spinal fracture. Flipping on the overhead light, he glanced at his watch. Nearly two in the morning.

J.C. dressed quickly, then wrote a note for Chrissy. Still uneasy with leaving her alone, he stopped at Blair's apartment, knocking quietly.

Yawning, she rubbed her eyes. "I'll try to listen, but I pulled a double yesterday and I'm beat."

"Sorry I woke you."

She yawned again. "Me, too."

"Thanks, Blair."

Still yawning she closed the door.

Once at the hospital, J.C. rushed to the trauma area. Fortunately, the situation wasn't as dire as he expected, but it was still over two hours before he neared home.

Red lights flashed from an ambulance, strobing eerily in the darkness. Grabbing his bag, he ran toward an EMT. *Chrissy! Had something happened to her?* "I'm a doctor." Panting, he caught his breath. "What's the situation?"

"Heart attack. Nurse that lives here gave him CPR. Touch and go, but she kept him alive."

"Nurse?" *Blair?* J.C. skirted the back of the ambulance, catching sight of Blair, then reaching her on a run. "Where's Chrissy?"

Blair looked distracted. "In your apartment I imagine. Had my hands pretty full here."

"Sorry. Of course." He pushed one hand through his thick hair. "Saved his life, I hear."

"Hope so."

J.C. loped across the lawn toward his apartment. Even from a distance, he could see that the overhead light in the living room was on. Not breaking his stride, he burst inside. But the living room was empty. With the lights on, his earlier tangle with the lamp looked ominous. "Chrissy?"

No answer.

The bedroom light was off, but he could see the mound of little girl beneath the covers. He switched on the lamp. "Chrissy?"

Muffled cries penetrated her covering.

Gently he peeled back the duvet. "It's okay."

"Uh-uh." She cried harder.

"I know one of the neighbors got sick, but it looks like he'll be all right."

"You weren't here!" she accused.

"There was an emergency—" J.C. started to explain.

"The sirens came and everything!"

Logic couldn't overcome her fear. "I'm here now."

Chrissy burst into a new round of tears. It was too late. And it wasn't enough. Worse, he couldn't promise it wouldn't happen again.

J.C. glanced at Lillian Carter's chart. "No nausea or decreased appetite?"

Maddie answered for her mother. "Nope. If anything, she's eating a bit more."

"Now is that something we tell handsome young men?" Lillian fussed, then smiled at J.C. To Maddie's surprise he didn't smile back. Wasn't like him. Not at all. Lillian smoothed her skirt. "You bake a lot of sweets. They're hard to resist."

"I do have a sweet tooth," Maddie admitted.

Again no reaction from J.C. Had they somehow irritated him? "Everything all right?"

"Hmm." Distracted, he glanced up from the chart. "I'm sorry, what?"

She frowned. "I said, is everything all right?"

He shrugged, then exhaled. "Not really."

She searched his expression. "Chrissy?"

J.C. explained the emergency call and his neighbor's heart attack.

"That's dreadful!"

"Chrissy's inconsolable."

"Of course," Lillian spoke up, surprising both of them. "A child must always feel safe. It's the parents' job to make sure of that."

Maddie wanted to wince for him. Still... "It's hard to hear, but true. J.C., you need help. And frankly, Mom and I could use the babysitting money."

"In the middle of the night?" he responded.

"Middle of the night, morning, after school, whenever we're needed. We don't exactly have a schedule carved in stone. You can drop Chrissy by if you get a call in the night. It's not ideal, but it's far better than leaving her alone."

He glanced at Lillian. "You have more to consider than just Chrissy."

"Do you have any tea, young man?" Lillian questioned, apparently now off the subject at hand.

J.C. sharpened his gaze. "No, Mrs. Carter, but I'm pretty sure your daughter does." He pushed the office intercom. "Didi? Could you bring in a cup of coffee for Mrs. Carter?"

"Sure, boss."

There was a soft knock on the exam room door, then Didi pushed it open. As she brought the coffee and tray with creamer and sugar, J.C. took Maddie's elbow, steering her to the other side of the room.

"Have you thought any more about your tea shop?"

Puzzled, she shook her head. "You know I can't—"

"You want a shop. I have a building that needs a tenant. More important, I have a niece who needs someone besides me in her life. She looks at every housekeeper and nanny I've hired as a threat, someone set up to take her mother's place. But she likes you. She likes Lillian." He glanced over at the older woman. "You have to admit your mother couldn't threaten a bug."

"But—"

"Chrissy wants to live in the building on Main Street."

Maddie blinked.

J.C. told her about the two apartments above the business level. "They haven't been lived in for a while. Jay's parents lived in one until they passed away. Then Jay used them mostly for storage the past few years, but both could be made livable without a lot of work."

"Even if that was a viable option, Mom can't handle stairs."

"Jay had an elevator put in for his parents."

Maddie glanced over at her mother who was busily chatting with Didi about African violets. "Even so…"

"It would be an enormous help to me. You and your mother are right. Chrissy should feel safe. With you directly across the hall, she would."

"We have our house…" Maddie tried to think of all the considerations.

"You mentioned needing money. Renting it out would give you a nice income. Not to mention what you make in the shop."

"I've told you, I don't have the money to start a business."

"Let me be your silent partner. Wagner Hill House has been a worry. I don't want it rented by some cheesy tourist outfit or chain restaurant. And if the building sits empty too long, it won't be good for the town."

Overwhelmed, Maddie stared at him. "Just like that? Up and move? Start a business with no money?"

"Just like that," he replied calmly. "What are your concerns?"

"Endless. My mother—"

"Would benefit from more interaction with people. That's a medical opinion."

She waved her hands in the air. "Fixing up the apartments."

"I have friends in the contracting business. Next."

"Renting out our house."

"I have a friend in real estate."

She plopped her hands on both hips. "Don't tell me, you have a friend in tearooms, as well?"

His eyes softened a fraction. "I hope so."

Her heart did a little two-step that dried her throat. "It's so much to take in."

"It's trite, but every journey begins with a step. Think Sam might stand in for you while we take a look at the apartments?"

"I suppose, but—"

"Good. How about tomorrow morning?"

"Tomorrow?" she couldn't keep the shock from her voice.

The smile she remembered was back on his face. "Unless you want to see them tonight?"

By morning, Maddie decided she was out of her mind. A sleepless night only confirmed the diagnosis. Now, a few hours later, Sam was perched on one of the kitchen chairs while Maddie turned on the electric kettle.

"I think it's a great idea!" Sam nibbled on a cookie. "I hope you plan to stock these. I could eat a dozen by myself."

Maddie rubbed her forehead, wondering why she'd given in to J.C.'s suggestion to phone Sam and set up the late-morning meeting. "You've just put at least a dozen carts before the horse. The more I think about J.C.'s idea—"

"Then stop thinking. Maddie, he's right. It's a good solution for all of you. J.C. needs help. Chrissy needs some stability in her life. Your mother will blossom—you know how she loves company. And you..."

"Can't finish that one, can you?"

"Actually I can, but you're too prickly right now to listen."

"Prickly?"

"You're not a martyr. I know that. But you're refusing to think beyond today. You're cutting corners now. How many are left? Do you see the cost of living shrinking in the next decade? And even though we don't want to think about it, Lillian's medical expenses could rise significantly. A business could give you the means to make sure you can take care of her. And, stubborn friend, what's wrong with *you* having some happiness? Pursuing your dream?"

Maddie swallowed. She'd purposely pushed their financial future to the corners of her thoughts, hoping that somehow it would work out. "And if the business is a big flop?"

Sam shook her head gently. "I doubt that's possible. But if it did, we'd be here for you—your friends, your neighbors."

Sighing Maddie plunked down into a chair across from her friend. "This is all going too fast. I barely know J.C."

"That could change," Sam suggested hopefully.

Maddie swallowed. That was about the scariest part of the whole venture.

J.C. was highly aware of Maddie's reluctance. He'd all but dragged her from her house. Feeling like a used car salesman, he'd talked up the place during the short drive to Main Street. Now, he inserted the key in the lock. Unused since Jay's death, the building seemed to echo with the loss. Jay's employees had scattered. Some were old enough to retire, the rest had found other jobs when the company closed. Without Jay's networking, the place would have crawled to a halt, so J.C. had chosen the only practical option.

Still, their footsteps rang in the emptiness.

"What happened to the equipment?" Maddie whispered.

"Sold it." His voice seemed unnaturally loud in the quiet. Finding a multiple light switch, he flipped all the levers. Fluorescent lights glared overhead. Seeing Maddie wince, he turned all but one off. "You'd have to imagine it without the commercial additions." He pointed toward the walls on the east side. "The original moldings are still in place. Jay updated the lighting and wiring for his business. But Wagner Hill House was built in the 1890s."

Maddie glanced around uncertainly. "The wood

floors are still good." She stared upward at the ugly drop ceiling.

"The original's still under those panels. Be easy to restore. Of course you have to look past the dust."

Just then she sneezed.

"*Way* under the dust."

"Seems more suited to a different sort of business." She halted in front of a stack of boxes taller than she was. "Not really a tea shop sort of place."

J.C. pointed to the original bay window that faced Main Street. "Picture it without the signs and printing displays. You could put up some kind of curtains, I imagine."

"Hmm." Maddie studied the large window. "European," she murmured. "That's the feel I always wanted. Plastered walls."

Helpfully, he gestured toward the original plastered walls. "They're still in good shape."

"Maybe..."

"Plumbing's good. You can reconfigure it however you want."

Maddie frowned. "Sounds expensive."

"That's where your silent partner comes in."

"I'd never be able to pay you back!"

"Look at it this way, Maddie. No matter who I rent to, I'm looking at renovations."

She looked at him suspiciously. "Are you sure?"

"Yep. And the improvements are a write-off. Just

clearing the rest of the junk out of here will make a big difference. You'll see."

Pivoting, she studied the space. "It would, actually."

"Let's take a look at the apartments. The elevator's in the back and there are two sets of stairs, one up front and one in the rear."

Reaching the front stairway, Maddie smoothed her hand over the curved bannister. "Lovely woodwork. Don't see this in modern buildings."

Her eyes were dusky gray in the muted light. Despite the reluctance in them, he spotted a vulnerable flicker of hope. He wondered how her face would look lit up with another emotion, a more personal feeling.

"Something wrong?"

Shaking his head, he smiled. "Just thinking of possibilities."

Upstairs, they entered the first apartment. Furniture shrouded in sheets were ghostly reminders of past occupants. J.C. opened long, heavy drapes that hid blurry windows. "Needs updating, of course."

"And a good clean." Maddie pulled a drop cover off the kitchen counter, revealing a beautiful dark green marble. "These are nice."

"I know in general the whole building looks dismal—I haven't spent any time here since Jay and Fran died. But Chrissy's right. It doesn't have the sad feeling their house does."

"Once it's cleared and cleaned, it will look a world better," Maddie encouraged. "Any place that's abandoned looks it."

"Guess we can take turns encouraging each other," he teased.

She grinned, then sobered. "True, but I don't want you to feel you have to bail me out. I know our situation isn't the best—"

"Agreed. Mine, either. Pooling our resources can fix that." He shoved the drapes open as far as they would go. "Imagine once the windows are clean, the walls have a fresh coat of paint, the place won't look so grim."

"I don't suffer from lack of imagination," she confessed. "Just the opposite, I'm afraid. I can close my eyes and see the shop of my dreams. I can also see the price tag. You're offering to be incredibly generous, but—"

"What? You'll go on the same way until you run out of money? Chrissy will get sadder, more out of control?"

Concern colored her eyes and blue now tinted the gray. "You're pushing my softie buttons."

"Is it working?"

"You swear that helping Chrissy will actually offset the cost of renovating the building? Of setting up the business?"

He fashioned the fingers of his right hand into the Boy Scout pledge. "Yep."

"I've always been a sucker for Boy Scouts."

"Really?"

Maddie suddenly looked embarrassed. "They're nice to old people." She gripped the strap on her shoulder bag. "Well, since we've decided, I guess we'd better break the news to Chrissy and my mother."

Apparently she didn't want him to press her personal buttons. "Right. I'll talk to Seth about the renovations. He can arrange for the cleanup, as well. I can talk to Paul Russell about leasing your house, if you want."

"So we're really doing this?" Worry pushed the blue from her eyes, rendering them the gray of clouds just beginning to darken.

"Yeah, we really are."

Chapter Six

Maddie added another note to her growing list. It still didn't seem real, but Paul Russell was already sending prospective tenants over to look at the house. His wife, Laura, had volunteered to come along and visit with Lillian whenever Paul showed the house. Maddie hated to depend on so many people, but the offer was helpful because she needed to make some measurements in both the new shop and apartment. Because of Chrissy, speed was imperative.

She'd told her mother about the plans, but like anything new that happened, Lillian couldn't retain the information. However, as usual, she loved having company.

Laura held up the tea cozy Lillian was crocheting. "I love this yarn. It feels soft enough for a baby."

Maddie mouthed *thank you,* then waved goodbye. With Laura chatting to her mother, Maddie hopped in her car and sped to Main Street. Ever since she'd agreed to the arrangement, a seed of excitement had begun blossoming. As she pulled into one of the diagonal spots out front, she saw window washers set up to clean the second-story windows. J.C. wasn't wasting a minute.

The bay window had already been scrubbed, all the old lettering removed, as well. Gleaming in the noonday sun, the glass practically winked an invitation. And she realized that the neglected limestone had been power washed, as well. Suddenly it was easy to imagine her shop, with its wide awning, pots of flowers and bistro tables out front.

Unwilling to build her hopes too high, she hesitantly opened the front door. The clutter was gone and workmen were pulling down the ugly ceiling panels. More dust and debris were being generated, but in a good way. The newly cleaned window allowed the light to pour inside, illuminating every nook and corner.

The kitchen should be in the back, centered so it had easy access, she decided. And shelves of tea blends should be off to the right so the inside tables could be placed front and center, beckoning guests to linger.

Dust motes floated through the sharp sunbeams, enticing her to spin slowly around in the near-empty room. The workers' voices faded as she imagined customers sharing the latest news, laughing as the tea worked its magic, carrying away the stress of the day.

As she revolved back to where she'd begun, she met J.C.'s gaze.

How had he come to be there? she wondered. She hadn't heard his footsteps. Lost in her thoughts, she'd forgotten she was smack dab center in the work area. Trying to recover some of her aplomb, she gestured toward the rear. "Just thinking about how everything should be laid out."

"Must have been good thoughts," he replied, the flecks in his brown eyes seeming to sweep right through her.

"Place is shaping up," she blurted. "The window—" pausing, she pointed to the bay window as though he might have missed it "—looks great. I can picture the awning, the tables out front."

"Just stopped by to see how it's coming. Seth says the bones are so good that it won't take long to fix things up. Have you talked to him about what you want?"

Want? She never thought about what she wanted. It occurred to her that since J.C. had come into her life, the possibility had flirted with her good sense. Was it somehow possible? Could what she wanted somehow be able to happen?

"The plans," J.C. reminded her. "I told Seth you choose the design, the materials, whatever you want. The shop and the apartments."

"Yes, the plans." She landed back on earth with a mental thud loud enough to shake away her wanderings.

"Do you know Seth McAllister? The contractor?"

"I don't think so. The name's familiar..." Glancing up toward the second story, she tried to shake off the distraction J.C. caused. "I haven't thought too much about the apartments, mostly just the shop so far."

"Seth says the plumbing and electric are all in good shape. As you saw, the kitchens and bathrooms in the apartments are, shall we say, quaint?"

She grinned. "I'm used to quaint. Oh, about Chrissy's bedroom—how about letting her have a big say in the decorating?"

J.C. shrugged. "Fine with me. I know even less about decorating girls' bedrooms than raising them."

"Her favorite color's purple. A soft lavender would really freshen her space."

"You can paint the whole thing purple," he agreed.

Looking into his eyes she sensed he wasn't thinking one bit about color. "I might just do that."

"Okay."

He definitely had something else on his mind. "Something going on?"

J.C. hesitated, which he seldom did.

"There you are!" a man called out. "I've had more luck chasing down prairie dogs."

J.C. turned around. "Seth. You need to meet Maddie, she's the one who'll be calling the shots."

"Not really—" she began, shaking the stranger's hand. "Nice to meet you. I just stopped by to take some measurements."

"Have time to look at the preliminary plans?" Seth carried tall cylinder rolls of paper in his hands. "I have a few configurations, but everything's changeable at this stage."

J.C. cupped her elbow and she swallowed at her unexpected reaction.

"That's Maddie's cue," he was saying. "All I care about is having two bedrooms in my apartment so I don't have to sleep in the living room. My spine's close to being permanently bent in the shape of a sofa."

J.C. took his hand away and immediately she felt disappointed.

"I'd better get back to the office," J.C. explained. "Got a full roster waiting."

Seth nodded in his direction, then turned to Maddie. "So," Seth began, "I hear we're going to build a tearoom and shop."

She pulled her gaze away from J.C.'s retreating back. "Yes…" Her voice was hoarse so she cleared her throat.

"J.C. told me about the general idea, but I imagine you're the one with the specifics." He chuckled. "My wife, Emma, always has the specifics."

Despite the storm of issues clouding her mind, the name penetrated. "Emma? Emma McAllister?"

"The very same."

"She owns the costume shop! My mother and I volunteered one year to make costumes for a school play." It had been the last year Lillian could concentrate long enough to complete even a small portion of a project. Maddie had assembled all the costumes in the final stage, but her mother had enjoyed prepping sleeves and tunics.

"Emma's assistant manager runs the shop now. Our kids keep Emma pretty busy these days."

"Of course." Other lives moved on, changed. Her own had been static so long that she often forgot that things were no longer the same for everyone else.

Seth placed a plank over two sawhorses to create a desklike area to spread the plans on. "These are computer-generated, so feel free to scribble away." He handed her a drafting pencil.

For a few moments she studied what he'd designed. "Is this a counter?"

"I'm thinking marble. Not big enough to compete with the old one at the drugstore." Rosewood's drugstore still held the original marble fountain from the last of the nineteenth century. The ice-cream creations produced at the area's oldest operating soda fountain lured people from the entire state.

"Hmm. I do want an old-world look for the shop. Maybe Carrera marble?"

He agreed and she went on to explain the custom shelving she wanted to hold jars of loose tea blends and numerous accessories. She envisioned decorating with all the teapots she'd wanted to buy but never had room to store.

"I agree with the location for the kitchen," Seth said as he penciled in a note. "Cutting-edge restaurants these days want to put the kitchen on display, but I didn't think that would work in this setting."

She laughed. "I like to cut the crusts off my sandwiches in private."

"And J.C. said you want to keep the original walls."

Nodding, she walked closer to see them in the sunlight, running her hand over the ageless plaster. "After they're painted, I want to apply a glaze. That won't take too long, will it?"

"Nope. Won't change our target completion date. I know how important it is to get the place renovated as soon as possible. Wouldn't want to leave my kids alone at night, either." Seth glanced again at the plans, making another note. "Place should look good. Emma can't wait to visit once you're up and running. Of course she'll have to drag the kids along."

"Kids?" Maddie mused, her thoughts whirling.

"Yep. They're her appendages."

Like most young women. "Seth, do you think we could work in a spot that would accommodate a few small tables—kid-size? Mothers would probably enjoy the convenience." Her mind flew into hyper-speed. "And maybe even little tea parties for birthdays. If we could fit it close to the corner for my mother, she'd love it. She adores children and they take to her."

Seth scribbled a few notes on the plans. "Don't see why not. Thinking of any built-ins for that area?"

Maddie rubbed her forehead. "I don't know yet."

"I'll work up another set of plans with the additions. Before the final decisions, we have plenty of demolition left to do. With the exception of plumbing and wiring, some things can be decided along the way."

Relieved, she exhaled. "That's good to hear. My mind's pretty full."

"Imagine so. What with setting up a business, moving, it's a lot to take on." His kindly gaze was calming.

"Thanks for understanding." She sensed it would be easy to work with Seth, which would ease some of her worry. Glancing at the now-vacant space where J.C. had stood, Maddie also sensed some of the anxiety was only going to increase.

"Are we really going to move to Dad's building?" Chrissy persisted.

She had asked the same question dozens of times since he'd told her about his plan. J.C. glanced up from the notes he was typing on his laptop. "I know I haven't done that great a job so far, but I've never lied to you."

"I didn't mean that." Chrissy picked at her light brown hair. "It's just that…"

She hadn't been able to count on anything since her parents' deaths. "Seth is working as fast as possible. We can stop by and see the progress if you like."

Chrissy tipped her head, considering. "Nah. That's okay. I kinda think I'd like to see it all fixed up." She didn't look completely convinced.

"What is it?"

"How come Maddie's going to move there? I mean, she's not family or anything."

Oh, she was definitely something. "I explained to you about how she's wanted to open a tea shop and that she and her mother need help."

"Oh."

"What?"

Chrissy shrugged. "Mrs. Lillian's pretty cool."

J.C. pulled his gaze from the computer. "This move will be good for her. With her type of dementia, interaction with people helps."

She frowned.

"Having you around will help her," he explained.

"She never tells me what to do."

Lifting his eyebrows, he studied his niece. "We all have rules and boundaries we have to live by."

She stuck out her lip.

"Your parents gave you rules."

Chrissy's lip wobbled, but her voice remained belligerent. "They were my *parents*."

And that was the rub. Having a bachelor uncle

as her only viable relative wasn't helping. He and Chrissy had always gotten on well together. But that was when he was her fun uncle, not her full-time guardian. "Do I make you follow more rules than they did?"

She shrugged.

It would be the most he'd get out of her on the subject. She had resented every nanny, housekeeper and babysitter he had hired and her behavior had driven each one of them away. He had explained over and over again that they weren't intended to replace her mother, but she refused to cooperate. "Chrissy, would you like to design your own room?"

Her brow scrunched in wary concentration. "What do you mean?"

"Maddie mentioned that she'd like your help in planning it."

"What about Mrs. Lillian?"

"I imagine Maddie could bring her mother along to add her ideas."

Chrissy studied him, then finally nodded. "I guess that'd be all right."

J.C. hid a grin. His niece looked intrigued. Good. When she saw that it was real, maybe she could begin the journey back to who she had been. He'd had another call from the principal. Chrissy was close to failing two subjects. He hated to think how he was letting his sister down.

* * *

True to his word, Seth and his crew were making great strides with the renovation. At J.C.'s request, Maddie and her mother had picked up Chrissy from school and taken her with them to Wagner Hill House. The girl waited while Maddie unloaded Lillian's wheelchair and got her settled into it. Together, they entered through the tall front door.

"Wow," Chrissy murmured as she took in all the changes on the first floor. She clutched her pink backpack tight.

Even though she was not a child and hadn't lost both parents, Maddie clearly remembered the loss of her own father. The feeling reinforced how all-consuming Chrissy's loss had been. She stopped beside the child. "It's pretty different. What do you think?"

Craning her head to look up, Chrissy tried to take in all the changes. "The ceiling looks kinda good."

"I think so, too," Lillian chimed in. "How did it look before?"

While Maddie explained, Chrissy strolled around the converted space, finally coming back to stand beside Lillian.

"The machines are all gone," Chrissy said in a small voice.

"Of course," Lillian replied. "Maddie doesn't need machines to make tea."

Maddie watched Chrissy, hoping the child wasn't

too overwhelmed. "Do you think your parents would like the changes?"

Chrissy shrugged. In the same small voice, she replied, "Maybe my mom."

"Everyone should enjoy tea," Lillian responded. "But it's usually women you'll find in a tearoom."

"Hopefully, because I'm selling loose tea blends, we'll get a few male customers, as well." Sensing the apartments would be less emotional for Chrissy, Maddie led them over to the elevator. "This is sure going to come in handy."

"My grandma used the elevator," Chrissy volunteered. "But that was a long time ago."

It was an unlucky stroke of fate that had also left Chrissy without grandparents.

"Would you like to push the button?" Maddie asked. "I haven't used this elevator yet."

Obligingly Chrissy pushed the button going up.

Maddie noticed a button marked *B*. "Does this actually go down to the basement?"

"Uh-huh. There's not much down there, though."

"Probably the furnace," Maddie mused.

On J.C.'s instructions, the apartments had been cleared. Although there was still some familiarity to her grandparents' place, J.C. had worried that it, too, contained memories of people Chrissy loved. He wanted a fresh start. Seth had suggested that after rebuilding the kitchens and bathrooms, they keep the original oak floors in the living, dining and bedroom areas. The other rooms were all in good shape, needing only a fresh coat of paint.

The main entry doors to both apartments were propped open, as well as the back ones that led out from the kitchens. Maddie followed as Chrissy walked into the apartment that had been her grandparents'.

"It looks so different." Her voice was still quiet but held a note of surprised interest.

"The kitchen and bathrooms will be all new." Maddie leaned down next to her mother. "We'll have a wheel-in shower in your bathroom. There's so much space, we each get our own private bathroom." One of the advantages of the old building, the apartments were generous in size. Seth confirmed that adding extra bathrooms would also add value to the property. "Oh, and Mom, the doorways will all be widened."

Chrissy looked back at Lillian. "That's good."

Maddie smiled, seeing the kindness J.C. had always insisted the child possessed. She had sensed the quality was there, but it was heartening to see her old traits reemerging.

"We don't need anything fancy," Lillian began. "But it never hurts to shake things up."

Unexpectedly Chrissy giggled.

Lillian had broken the tension in a way Maddie couldn't have managed.

"You're right, Mom. I'm excited about having a new kitchen."

"Imagine what you can brew up, then," Lillian replied tartly. "Maybe even some magic."

"Magic?" Maddie chuckled deprecatingly. Her mother meant romance. Not much chance.

Lillian wheeled her chair toward the large front window. Reaching the sill, she glanced out. "We'll be right in the center of the action."

Chrissy giggled again, lingering beside Lillian, relaxing.

Maddie noticed buckets and wall cleaner sitting in one corner. Glancing upward, she saw what looked like smoke stains on the ceiling. Unless there'd been a fire… She looked closer at the wall. The finish was smooth, unlike the other plaster walls. As she tapped lightly, the sound went from solid to hollow. Intrigued, she wondered what laid beneath the surface.

Lillian and Chrissy headed toward the first bedroom. Reluctantly, Maddie left the discovery behind.

"Is this going to be my bedroom?" Chrissy asked, crossing over to the window seat.

"Your uncle said for you to choose."

"This one," she decided, scooting deeper into the window nook.

"Good choice," Lillian declared. "Nothing like a window seat to read a good book."

"Or to dream in," Maddie added quietly.

Chrissy's gaze darted toward hers, a flash of understanding in her eyes.

Maddie smiled, but Chrissy turned away, her defenses back up.

Not taking it personally, Maddie glanced around the room. "Tell me again what your favorite colors are."

"I used to like pink," Chrissy replied.

Maddie hid her smile. Nine years old and trying to be twice her age. "Me, too. Do you remember telling me that you like purple?"

"I guess."

Maddie had gone to the hardware store for color chip samples and she pulled one from her pocket. "What do you think of these shades?"

Chrissy glanced over. Then, drawn by the sample card, inched closer. Finally she pointed to one of the colors at the top of the card. "That one's okay."

"With crisp white trim?"

"I guess."

"She'll need curtains," Lillian inserted as she dug in her purse. "And a new bedspread."

"And furniture," Maddie added.

Chrissy's determinedly sullen expression vanished. "I get new furniture?"

"Your uncle wants you to pick all new things."

Lillian beamed, offering a butterscotch Life Saver to Chrissy. "Aren't you a lucky girl?"

Maddie winced inwardly at her choice of words, but Chrissy didn't seem to mind. "*All* new?"

"That's what he said."

Slowly Chrissy twirled in the center of the room, Lillian watching in delight.

Maddie met her mother's gaze. It was probably her imagination, but it seemed as though she glimpsed a bit of the past in Lillian's nostalgic gaze. Maybe, just maybe, J.C. was right. This move might be good for her mother. Sending a silent prayer toward heaven, she held the hope close.

Chapter Seven

A month later, Maddie stood in front of her new shop watching as the awning was being installed. The Edwardian building suited the furnishings and accoutrements she'd chosen. As the fabric of the awning unfurled, her eyes swept over the exquisite lettering: *Tea Cart*.

Perfect.

Inside, she had envisioned elegant, delicate, inviting. Hoping to achieve that look, she'd brought many of the furnishings from home. The collection of family antiques that she and Lillian had simply considered furniture mixed with new pieces. With Chrissy's agreement, she'd brought a small table to sit beside the front door. It would hold menus and mints.

A van pulled into one of the parking places on the street. Maddie turned, recognizing Samantha's business van, Conway's Nursery. Sam climbed out of the driver's seat, then headed toward the rear of the van.

Curious, Maddie followed.

Sam propped open one of the rear doors, then reached inside. As Maddie watched, Sam pulled out a charmingly weathered terra-cotta pot filled with what appeared to be a miniature Christmas tree.

"Dwarf Alberta spruce," Sam explained, touching the soft grass-green needles. "It'll look like this year-round. No dead-brown in the winter."

"Sam, it's gorgeous, but I didn't buy—"

"Housewarming present," Sam replied briskly. "And you can refuse until you're hoarse, but it won't do you any good."

Knowing her friend meant business, Maddie gave in gracefully. "It's lovely. Thank you."

Sam plopped the container in Maddie's hands. "By the door, I think."

Maddie decided her friend was right. The dwarf spruce looked perfect by the door. She turned to say so and noticed that Sam hadn't emerged from behind the van. "Sam?" Not getting an answer, she returned to see that her friend had the other rear door propped open, as well.

Sam held a matching container. "For the other side of the door."

"But—"

"So this doesn't take all day, look inside."

Cautiously Maddie peered into the van. The floor was filled with all sorts of container plants. "And?"

"They're for you."

"I really can't—"

"You never let us help you as much as we'd like with Lillian. I know you think Bret and I can't spare the time, or should use it to be with each other, but we'd like to help, really help."

Wordless, Maddie stared at her friend.

"So, you going to help me get them positioned?"

"I—" A rush of emotion choked her throat.

Sam took the opportunity to plop the second container in her hands. "The other side of the door."

While Maddie carried the matching spruce to the door, Sam pulled several other containers forward. "Just grab what's next," she instructed, carrying a hanging wire basket filled with overflowing gardenias and jasmine. Despite her cane, she managed almost effortlessly. "I want to set things out before we hang these, see if how I designed it works as well as it did on paper."

Maddie moved the remainder of the potted evergreens from the van, marveling at each species, loving the way they were coming together.

"*Koreana.* Also known as Korean boxwood, although the chain nurseries don't always label boxwood correctly. The California Korean boxwood is a completely different animal, so to speak." Sam traced her fingers over one of the glossy dark leaves. "You said you wanted a European look, so I tried for something between an English cottage garden and an Italian terrace." The boxwood spilled over the pot, draping over the aged terra-cotta to touch the brick pavement.

Maddie frowned. "I don't remember ever seeing anything like these at your nursery." Conway's specialized in native species.

"Computer and a phone—a person can order most anything these days. The flowers are all local, if that makes you feel better."

Maddie grinned. "I'm not the one committed to conserving our corner of Texas, as you and Bret phrase it."

Sam muttered something under her breath as she repositioned the white cedar. The delicately textured bluish-green foliage was a breathtaking contrast to the boxwood. "Why don't you make yourself useful and grab a ladder. I need to position the climbing ivy. Once we get it attached, I don't want to have to move it."

"Aye, aye." Maddie knew exactly where the stepladder was because she'd used it constantly over the past few weeks to stock her shop. Taking the ladder outside, she set it up quickly. "This thing's become another appendage." She loved the look of the scaled-down Christmas trees. "How tall do these get?"

Sam turned to the four-foot plants. "These are fairly mature shrubs. Takes thirty-five years for them to grow to seven feet."

"Wow. Individually the plants are great. All together, they're gorgeous. I had planned to add plants at some point, but I wouldn't have known how to design anything like this."

"That's why I'm the botanist," Sam replied with a cheeky grin. "How much longer until your grand opening?"

"I'm not sure. We're concentrating on the apartments first so we can get Chrissy settled. Mom and I have a tenant for the house and we've been packing for the last month. A lot will go into storage, which is fine. And I cherry-picked the antiques I want to use in the shop. It's all still hard to believe."

Samantha's smile softened. "It is, isn't it?"

"What are you doing?" a loud male voice intruded.

Startled, both women turned to stare at Owen Radley, Maddie's former fiancé.

"I asked what you're doing," Owen demanded, his thick body bristling.

Maddie squinted, then shook her head, feeling she needed to clear her vision or her mind, maybe both. He had cropped his blond hair so short, his scowling face looked rounder than she remembered. The years hadn't been especially kind. She didn't remember the deep creases beside his thick lips, or the lines around his pale blue eyes. "What?"

"That's what I asked you." There was nothing soft in his face or voice. When he was younger, Owen had been sensitive. Apparently, after years of being in the business world, he had abandoned any such notions. A small part of her mourned its passing. "Well?" he insisted.

"Well what?"

Impatience flashed in his eyes, pulled down the corners of his mouth. "What's wrong with you, Maddie? I asked what you're doing."

"Why does it concern you?" Sam interjected.

"I wasn't speaking to you," he replied abruptly. "What's between Maddie and me isn't any of your concern."

Samantha raised her eyebrows, then swung her gaze to meet Maddie's.

Knowing exactly what her friend was thinking, Maddie heard the echo of Owen's words. *What's between Maddie and me.* "Owen, what are you talking about?"

He waved to the new awning. "Tea Cart is what you planned to call your tea shop," he accused.

She wondered at the anger that had him bristling. "Of course."

"So what's all this about? Has your mother passed on?"

Maddie flinched, hearing Sam gasp at the same time. Ice formed amid the unexpected hurt. "No."

Owen's frown deepened, and Maddie noticed the well-defined grooves in his skin that indicated he frowned often. "Then I don't understand."

"There's nothing to understand. I'm opening my tea shop."

His dark eyes narrowed. "You said you were devoting your life to taking care of your mother."

"I am."

Owen gestured to the shop. "This isn't a *small* conflict of interest."

Aggravated, she wondered why he had happened along to spoil her day. "Look, Owen—"

He glanced pointedly at Sam. "Does your friend have to hang around?"

Samantha leveled a glare that would have stopped bigger men. "Definitely."

"I expect an explanation, Maddie. When your bodyguard isn't around."

"I don't—"

But Owen was striding down the sidewalk.

"What blew the rat in?" Samantha wondered aloud.

Maddie shook her head. "No idea. I haven't seen him in…" She tried to think. "It's been so long I don't really know. *Explanation? Owen* wants an explanation?"

"Maybe you should send him to J.C."

"I can defend myself."

Samantha grimaced. "J.C.'s a neurologist, and Owen definitely needs his head examined."

Maddie chuckled in spite of herself. "I'm not sure J.C. would appreciate the referral."

Sam stared down the street. "He gives me the creeps."

"I was having such a good time…" Maddie shuddered. "You know that old expression—feels like someone's walking on my grave?"

"He'd be doing a jig." Sam frowned. "I don't like this."

"I'm sure it was a one-time hit-and-run."

Sam didn't stop staring at his retreating figure. "I'm not."

Reluctantly, Maddie joined her gaze. Owen was almost out of sight. She intended to make sure he was also out of mind.

J.C. stacked the last of the day's boxes in one corner of his bedroom. Seth had enlisted a second contractor and together their crews had worked in record time. The apartments were nearly ready. With Chrissy still crying herself to sleep each night, it wasn't a moment too soon.

Straightening up, he heard a noise from across the hall. Because no air-conditioning or heat was running, it was especially quiet in the building. J.C. glanced at his watch. Eight in the evening. All the workers should be gone. He'd left Chrissy with Maddie and Lillian. More curious than concerned, he crossed through his apartment and saw that the door to the other apartment was now open. Funny, he distinctly remembered it had been closed.

He hadn't locked the front door of the building, but crime was a nonissue in Rosewood. The most that ever happened were car accidents and teenage pranks. There had been one case of arson, but that had been solved and the culprit was behind bars.

Footsteps echoed over the oak floors, then a light flickered on.

Was someone just curious? But why poke around at night?

Hugging the wall, J.C. glanced inside. Nothing.

Thud.

Sounded like a box was dropped. Almost immediately, he heard something being dragged across the floor, something relatively heavy. J.C. wasn't innately suspicious, but what was someone up to? It couldn't be a workman; they were all gone for the day.

He still wore the soft-soled shoes that he'd had on during his hospital rounds. They made it easy for him to move silently as he closed in on the bedroom where the noise came from. Suddenly the light flickered off. *Maybe he hadn't been as quiet as he thought.*

J.C. stepped away from the wall, intending to block the intruder. As he did, he crashed into a body much softer than he expected.

A feminine scream made him jump back.

"It's J.C."

"What?" Maddie's breath was short, fear prickling her voice.

"It's me. J.C."

"Why are you creeping around in the dark? You

scared the life out of me." One hand pressed against her neck, the other against the wall.

"Last time I saw you was at your house, remember? Watching Chrissy?"

Her breath was coming back, but her eyes were still wide. "Yes, well, Sam and Bret came over. They're with our *ladies*. Sheesh. I thought I'd take the time to bring a few things over that I didn't want to move by truck." She pointed into the living room. "That vase has been in our family forever."

"I'm glad you weren't still carrying it. I have a feeling it might have landed on my head." Seeing the humor in the situation, he grinned.

She hesitated, then smiled, as well. "I guess I looked pretty ridiculous jumping out of my skin like that."

He tagged her wrist. "Looks intact."

Maddie chuckled. "You're okay for a boogeyman."

"Did you get all your *fragiles* moved?"

"Pretty much. Some of Seth's guys took the rest of the stuff marked for storage today. House looks… not bare, but unsettled. Then in two weeks…"

Moving day. They had plenty of volunteers lined up. Adam had even rearranged his schedule to help. J.C. wanted to move in immediately, but he had a full surgery schedule on Friday, which meant the coming Saturday was out. He was on call and had to be there for his postoperative patients. "Ready?"

"It's more change than I've experienced in a decade," she admitted.

"Is that bad?"

Maddie shook her head. "A little daunting."

"I'd offer a comforting cup of tea, but…"

She laughed, the reservation in her expression fading. "That part is amazing."

Her radiant eyes were a deep blue. And her lips parted in a smile, lighting up the rest of her face. Wanting to reach out and touch the curve of her cheek, he checked the motion, tucking his hands behind his back.

"I have a nearly finalized copy of my menu," she told him, heading toward the living room. Several paintings were stacked against the wall.

He nodded toward them. "Part of your *fragiles?*"

"My dad painted. Not professionally, but well, I think. I wanted to make sure nothing happened to them."

Bending down, J.C. picked up the one on top. Studying the canvas, he was surprised to see a portrait of a young Lillian. He sorted through the remainder. Most amateurs painted landscapes or still-life groupings. Not the late Mr. Carter. His subjects seemed to all be people. Grasping the next picture, he recognized a young Maddie. She must have been about sixteen. A very sweet sixteen.

A thud made him look up. Maddie was marking the wall.

"Let me help you with that," he offered. "Did you bring molly bolts—wall anchors—for the heavier paintings?"

She put down the hammer, then picked up an unopened package. "Yep."

He restacked the pictures he was holding and retrieved the hammer. Tapping on the wall, he looked for Maddie's markings.

She caught his elbow. "I'm not sure about this wall. I don't think it's…normal."

"In what way?"

Maddie knocked on the wall, starting as high as she could reach, then downward. It sounded solid at first, then he heard a hollow ringing. "It doesn't sound right, does it?"

"I never saw the apartments when they were lived in. We donated the paper stored up here, but even then I just took a quick glance around. Maybe something's been walled over."

Her expression brightened. "Like maybe a fireplace?"

"I suppose so. Why don't you check?"

Maddie blinked. "Knock a hole in the wall? I couldn't do that."

"I can." He tapped on the wall, but hit a solid structure.

"I think it's lower." Maddie stepped closer.

He swung the hammer, extending it out farther than he intended.

Maddie swivelled to avoid the claw end of the hammer, but started to slip on the newly polished floor.

Seeing that she was about to fall, J.C. reached for her. But the same slick floor tripped him up, too. Together they crashed into the wall. The ancient plaster connecting to the Sheetrock fractured under the pressure. As they tumbled, crumbs of falling plaster along with Sheetrock dust covered them. Pieces of the demolished Sheetrock rained down.

Afraid that Maddie would get hurt, J.C. pulled her close, shielding her from the landslide around them. Immediately aware of her softness, he caught his breath. Up close, he could smell the soft scent of apple blossoms from her hair. Silky hair slid beneath his hands.

His breath deepened. As though in accompaniment, hers did, too.

Arms still wrapped around her, he was close enough to see the blue in her eyes darken, her lips opening in a silent sigh. Tipping his head, he reached to close the distance, to see if her lips were as soft as they looked.

Unable to keep her reaction under control, Maddie pulled away. Trying to rein in her breathing, she jumped up. Disappointment flashed in J.C.'s face. But it disappeared so quickly Maddie wondered if she'd imagined it.

Although dust still sifted from the wall, she spotted what looked like granite. Using it as a distraction, she brushed some of the dust away, uncovering pinkish-red granite. "It *is* a fireplace!" she blurted out, scooting even farther away, hoping to disguise her awkward response to him.

"So it is. Good call."

Nervously, ran her hand over what remained of the wall. Sheetrock still clung to some of the stone, but the large fireplace was open. Over six feet tall, J.C. had to crouch to get out of the fireplace. Emerging, he swiped at the dust that coated his jeans.

My, his legs were long! Catching herself watching too intently, Maddie dusted her own cotton trousers again, even though she'd already wiped most of the debris away. She didn't know what to do with her hands or which way to look. Every direction seemed to contain a glimpse of J.C.

"I hope Seth won't be upset with what we did," she said in a strangled voice.

"Won't be too much work for his guys." J.C. ran his fingers over the jagged edges of remaining Sheetrock. "It'll look better with plaster."

"Do you suppose there's one, a fireplace I mean, in your apartment?"

"Probably."

She could tell he didn't want to talk about fireplaces, but she wasn't about to address her reaction to him. "I guess it would be too much to hope there's one downstairs."

"Did you check the walls?"

Maddie shook her head, not caring about fire-places, either. "J.C.?"

"Yes?"

What was she going to do—blurt out her thoughts? "Oh…nothing. Went out of my head. Guess I'd better get going."

"What about the paintings?"

"Paintings?"

He pointed to the pile of her father's portraits.

Feeling her cheeks go hot, she felt like an idiot. "We don't have to hang them now."

J.C. tilted his head in question.

"I mean…it will look different with the fireplace exposed. I'll have to think about where to put them. Are you going to see if there's a fireplace in your apartment?"

"Suppose so."

"Do you need any help?" she asked, even though she didn't want to repeat the experience. She might not be able to hide her response a second time.

"I can do it on my own."

"Oh. Of course." *Ridiculous, the letdown feeling.* "Then I'll say good-night."

Nodding, he walked out of the apartment to cross the hall. And Maddie couldn't help wishing he had asked her to stay.

Chapter Eight

～❧

After lunch at the café a few days later, J.C. decided to walk to what would soon be his new home. Although he'd tried to push Maddie from his thoughts, she remained there. Why had she reacted as she had? True, he was skeptical about another relationship himself, but Maddie had acted as though she'd touched fire, jerking away so abruptly.

Now that it was too late to undo their arrangement, he wondered if he had made the right decision. She would be living across the hall. And Chrissy would be spending a lot of time with her, further complicating things.

J.C. took a deep breath. There wasn't an alternative. Chrissy needed this. And for all he knew, Maddie had her reasons for backing off so quickly.

Activity at Wagner Hill House flurried. J.C. drew his eyebrows together as he watched the scene. Maddie stood out front and a man held her arm possessively. Walking closer, J.C. recognized him.

Owen Radley. The guy had an ego the size of his family's fortune.

J.C. could hear the sound of voices. If he kept approaching, he'd walk right into the middle of the duo. Pausing, he strained to make out their words. Owen repeated Maddie's name in a raised voice. But her tone didn't match his.

Watching closely, his protective instincts kicked in, surprising him. Maddie wasn't his responsibility. Still, he itched to yank Owen's hand from her arm.

Just then, Maddie stepped back and Owen loosened his grip. She rushed inside her shop. Owen strode quickly away in the other direction. J.C. wished the man had come toward him. He wanted to see his expression, witness whether Owen had a claim to Maddie.

The fact that he did halted his steps. J.C. didn't want those feelings again. His jaw tightened, remembering his ex-wife, Amy. Her cheating had nearly killed him. Once she left, he'd filled his life with his work and family. Pushing the inevitable loneliness to the back of his mind, J.C. had decided being lonely was preferable to the torment of betrayal.

Maddie had never mentioned Owen Radley. His gut tightened. Evidently, she had secrets of her own. As J.C. watched, the other man stopped next to a Cadillac Escalade, got in and roared off.

Memories hit like a bitter taste, unwelcome, hard

to get rid of. His ex-wife had possessed two faces, one that charmed, one that bit once he was lulled. He had dreamed of a family; Amy wanted only what made her happy—his money, her *interests*. Interests that he eventually learned consisted mostly of other men. She had bad-mouthed J.C. to her friends, claiming he was cold, uninterested in her. He supposed it made her cheating seem more acceptable to her way of thinking.

J.C. had been drawn to Amy because of her large personality and contagious sense of fun. He hadn't realized that both camouflaged a self-obsessed narcissist. The betrayal still cut deep. So deep he hadn't allowed himself to trust another woman. He had been so certain he knew Amy before they married, that she was the person he wanted to be with for the rest of his life. The scars she inflicted remained, reminders of how blind he'd been.

Lifting his gaze, J.C. stared down Main Street, Owen's flashy car now gone. Turning on his heel, he left the Wagner Hill House behind, wishing he could leave his thoughts as easily.

The first floor of the building was swept clean. It wasn't long now until moving day. Nervously, Maddie studied Chrissy's expression. Maddie had brought over an old painting which had hung in the living room of Chrissy's former home. The impressionist style scene was lighthearted—a Victorian couple dining in the dappled sunshine beneath the leafy branches of a chestnut tree.

Not seeing any consternation, Maddie touched the gilt frame. "I love the composition—that they're eating at a small round table." Pointing toward the partially assembled tearoom with its eclectic mix of tables where customers would hopefully soon be sitting, Maddie smiled. "Seems as though it was meant to be."

"I guess so."

Maddie knelt down. "Chrissy, if you don't want it here, I'll take it down. I hoped it would be a good memory, something that makes you feel at home."

Chrissy nodded. "It's okay."

Worried about her next surprise, Maddie offered her hand. "Will you come upstairs? I have something else to show you."

The child glanced in Lillian's direction where Maddie had set up a small television to keep her occupied. "Will Mrs. Lillian be okay?"

Touched by Chrissy's concern, Maddie squeezed her hand. "We'll only be a few minutes."

Given free rein by J.C., Maddie had chosen more contemporary pieces for his apartment. She hadn't wanted to drown Chrissy in the past, but she did want the home to feel cozy, so she warmed the walls with a classic but modern sage-green that complemented the oak floors. Maddie wasn't sure if he would, but J.C. had opened up the fireplace and it made a perfect focal point for the room.

Above it, Maddie hung a family portrait of Chrissy and her parents.

Not letting go of the child's hand, Maddie nudged her to look up over the mantel.

Feeling her hand tremble, Maddie drew Chrissy closer. "It's completely up to you whether the picture stays."

Chrissy stared, tears gathering in her eyes.

"Oh, sweetheart, I didn't mean to upset you! I'll take it down."

Maddie reached for the portrait and almost immediately Chrissy snagged her arm. "I miss my mommy and daddy."

Heart breaking for her, Maddie enveloped the child in a hug. "I know." Smoothing her light brown hair, Maddie wished she had more comfort to offer, something that could ease the pain.

Minutes passed before Chrissy pulled away, wiping at the tears on her cheeks.

"We don't have to decide about the portrait today."

Chrissy sniffled in reply.

"Shall we go check on…" Maddie had almost said *her mom*. Quickly she changed the term. "Mrs. Lillian? I brought sandwiches. Maybe she'll be hungry." And hopefully, Chrissy would eat, too. There had been so much change in her young life that Chrissy could seldom be coaxed to eat enough, and she had lost far too much weight for her small frame.

Back downstairs, Chrissy checked on Lillian,

who produced a roll of Life Savers, then companionably offered one to the girl. Maddie's worry eased a fraction. They were an unlikely pair, but Chrissy had latched onto Lillian. And Lillian responded in a way that made her seem a little more like her old self. If a stranger were to drop in at that moment, they might suppose that Lillian was fine. An incredible blessing.

Nearly as remarkable was the coming together of her shop. The shelves that Seth's carpenter built were exactly as she had envisioned. Apothecary jars filled with her own blends mingled with classics like Earl Grey that she had recently ordered. Tea shops were on the rise just as coffeehouses had once boomed. So her suppliers carried enough varieties to please anyone she could imagine.

Seth had built out her mother's nook perfectly. It wasn't far from the fireplace he had unearthed. And with plenty of room to pull up extra chairs, Lillian could interact with customers and friends. And next to that space was the one designated for the children's tables. The more she'd thought about it, the more Maddie wanted to offer tea parties for the younger set. She had already planned on carrying a line of sodas and other drinks as well as tea. And on the final menu, she had included kid-friendly sandwiches and desserts.

Among the teapots and mugs, Maddie had interspersed smaller versions for the children. As a young girl, she'd prepared many a tea party for her parents, friends, dolls and stuffed animals. She wasn't certain little girls still enjoyed having tea parties, but she gave in to the whimsy. If they caught on, she planned to offer "dress up" costumes and cake for birthday celebrations, the ultimate little girl's tea party.

Maddie glanced at her favorite purchase, a gleaming French 1940s iron-and-gilt rope three-tier tea cart, which would soon be filled with pastries and delicate sandwiches. Samantha had helped her find it online. Afraid that the cart might break in the shipping, Maddie had been delighted to see that all three glass shelves arrived intact, the frame unbent. *But what was that sitting on the top tier?*

Her menu? But it wasn't just a copy of her finalized menu. Framed in dark cherrywood, matted to match the ink, this was a piece of art. Instantly she remembered something J.C. had said after he'd admired the line sketches she had drawn on the menu. *When the menu is all set, you need to put up a framed copy.* She glanced again at the cart, but there was no note, no indication of how the piece had been delivered.

Easing her fingers over the delicately scrolled frame, Maddie wondered. And held on to a wish she had no business courting.

J.C. stopped by the Wagner Hill House after his hospital rounds a few evenings later. His last patient was an elderly man with rapidly advancing dementia. Reminded of Lillian, his thoughts turned far too easily to Maddie. The previous evening he had dreamed of Maddie and Owen Radley. Amy wove her way in between the two and his dream launched into a full-fledged nightmare. Although he carried the mistakes of his past with him every day, they hadn't enveloped him like this since his divorce.

Pushing open the front door, he noticed it wasn't locked. But the shop area was dark, the workers all gone. Last person out probably just forgot to lock it. Having grown up in a house that never had locked doors, it didn't bother him. Baylor Med in Houston had taught him that that wasn't a safe practice in the city, but this was Rosewood.

J.C. shifted the box he held and flipped on the light over the stairwell along with the second-floor hall light. Only days away from fully moving in, he wanted to see the final product. With most of their stuff packed, Chrissy was staying with Maddie and Lillian this last week until the move. From what he could get out of his niece, she seemed to like her new room.

The doors to both apartments were closed but not locked. Pushing open the one to his place, J.C. deposited the box on the dining room table. The living room was dotted with color, a far cry from his beige apartment.

Glancing past the kitchen, he saw that the doors were gone from the old butler's pantry. Curious, he switched on one of the lamps. Tucked into the spot was a scaled-down but complete study. Although accustomed to doing his paperwork on whatever bit of space was available on the coffee table or kitchen counter, he had needed a home office for years.

J.C. ran his hands over the smooth beech surface of the desk. What could have been a dark hole was light because of the wood and glass choices Maddie had made. *Why had she taken the time and trouble to convert the butler's pantry to a work area for him?*

His mind full, J.C. ambled out into the hall. He intended to enter only his own apartment, but his fingers closed around the doorknob of Maddie's place. Swinging open the door, he was met with silence. *What had he expected? Maddie? Waiting for him to just stumble by?* Feeling ridiculous, he turned to go.

Click.

It was a quiet sound, nearly inaudible. Had he imagined it? J.C. listened again.

Nothing.

A footstep whispered in the dining room close by. *Must be Maddie.* Not completely sure whether he wanted to run into her, he hesitated. Remembering how he had scared her before, J.C. flipped on the light switch, blinking at the sudden change.

Eyes focusing, they landed on the last person in the world he expected to see. Owen Radley. "What are you doing here?"

"I could ask you the same thing," Owen countered.

J.C. angled his head in disbelief. "I don't think so."

Owen's eyes narrowed into ugly lines. "Unless you own the place—"

"Actually, I do."

Owen didn't like being crossed and didn't mind showing it. "You *don't* own Maddie Carter."

J.C. felt a tic in his jaw and forced himself to be still. What was Owen implying? That he had a hold on Maddie?

Owen stood his ground, his posture and gaze a clear challenge.

J.C. didn't have a claim to Maddie, but he didn't have to allow Owen in the place. "I was just locking up."

Owen frowned, obviously resenting J.C.'s tone. Instead of replying, he pushed past J.C. and out the door.

Staring after him, J.C. wondered if Owen and Maddie… She had never said anything about him, still… The other man's attitude implied that Maddie *was* his business. He glanced at the short distance in the corridor between their apartments, and hated the sinking in his gut that told him he would learn soon enough.

Moving day was exhausting, but at the same time exhilarating. No longer running between Wagner Hill and the Carter home, Maddie would be able to devote more time to her shop, get it ready for her grand opening day. There wasn't that much left to do, but she wanted to make it perfect.

Even though friends were helping, J.C. had hired some men to carry the heavy furniture up the stairs. Maddie asked them to set up the beds first, including the extra twin bed in her own room that was for Chrissy whenever she stayed over. By the end of moving day, Maddie wanted to be certain everyone was able to sleep in his or her own bed.

Lillian was at Samantha's for the day because the stress of the move would be overwhelming. Maddie hadn't purchased any new furniture for their apartment, intending to set it up to resemble their home. Familiarity in their surroundings was important with Lillian's dementia. Blessedly, her mother still recognized her own home and possessions.

While the movers left to take a short break, Maddie quickly put sheets on all the beds, then added blankets and pillows. Nothing worse at the end of a grueling moving day than to find they were camping out instead of curling into their beds. As a final touch, she plumped the small heart-shaped pillow that her father had given her mother on their first anniversary.

"What's that?" Chrissy asked.

Startled, Maddie whirled around. "I didn't hear you come in. Whew! Um, this? It's a special pillow Mrs. Lillian likes to put on her bed."

"Oh."

"Is everything going all right at your end?"

Chrissy shrugged. "I guess."

"How about your room?" Maddie had drawn a scaled sketch of just where everything should be arranged so J.C. could tell the movers.

A sliver of interest pricked the girl's eyes. "It's okay."

"Need any help?"

"Nah."

"I'm planning to come over and make sure everything is set up right once all the furniture is delivered. That okay with you?"

The resolute lines in Chrissy's face eased. "Yeah."

She was trying so hard to be all grown up, but she was just a little girl. Impulsively, Maddie smoothed her ponytail. "I'm excited about being neighbors."

Chrissy snubbed the toe of her shoe at the floor. "Where's Mrs. Lillian?"

"She's at my friend Samantha's. You've met her."

"When will she be back?"

"Later today after the movers have gone."

Relief flashed in the child's eyes. "Good."

"My feelings exactly."

Chrissy lifted her face, her expression a trifle less guarded. "Does she like going to Samantha's?"

"Yes, but when she's tired she likes to be home. That's why I wanted to finish her bedroom first."

"How come you didn't get new furniture?"

If only life were that uncomplicated. "What we had is fine."

Chrissy scrunched her forehead in concentration. "The apartments are way different."

"Because people are different," Maddie explained. "My mother is comfortable in the furniture she picked out years ago. She'll have lots of new to get used to down in the shop."

"Oh."

Maddie glanced at her watch. "Are you getting hungry?"

Chrissy shook her head.

The child never wanted to eat. "What about your uncle?"

"I dunno."

Maddie needed to continue putting things away, but Chrissy had to eat some lunch. "Why don't we go check?"

Chrissy didn't reply, but she followed Maddie across the hall. Poking her head into the kitchen, Maddie felt a tap on her shoulder and let out a squeal before she saw that it was J.C. "You gave me a start."

J.C.'s expression flickered.

Instantly, she wondered if he, too, was remembering their encounter on the night they crashed into the fireplace.

"Looking for me?"

"Yes." Realizing she sounded breathless, Maddie calmed her voice. "Chrissy should eat some lunch."

J.C. pointed to the dining room table. "Ordered from the café. Just sandwiches and chips."

Maddie felt unreasonably nervous around him. "Then I'll leave you to it."

"I ordered enough for all of us."

"Oh." She noticed three paper drink cups, as well. The chairs were scattered around the spacious table and she was suddenly very glad that the old apartments were so large. Unlike most new ones, these had been built when families gathered around the table for every meal. So the dining room wasn't an abbreviation linked to the living room. Instead, there was plenty of room for them to spread out. Which Maddie did, taking the chair at the far end of the table.

"We've got ham and cheese, roast beef and pimento cheese," J.C. told her.

"Anything's fine." Maddie directed her attention to Chrissy. "What's your favorite?"

Predictably the child shrugged.

J.C. handed Chrissy a sandwich. "Ham and American cheese with mayo on plain white bread." Then he offered Maddie the other two sandwiches.

"Really, I don't care."

"You choose."

He seemed to be challenging her. Deciding she must be overly tired from not sleeping the previous night and imagining things, she opted for the pimento cheese. But J.C.'s eyes remained on her as she unwrapped the sandwich. Her own appetite dried up under his scrutiny. Chrissy glanced sideways at her, so Maddie made an effort. Although the pimento cheese sandwich was tasty, she felt as though she was trying to swallow cardboard. Unaccustomed to the intensity in his gaze, she wondered what could have caused it. Sipping soda from her cup, she tried to wash down the bite of sandwich. "Just think, not too long and we'll have cucumber sandwiches and tea right downstairs."

Chrissy looked at her blankly.

"Not just cucumber," Maddie rushed to explain and fill in the awkward silence. "We'll have all kinds of sandwich fillings. And pastries. And tea, of course." Both J.C. and Chrissy stared at her. "All kinds of teas," she ended lamely. She needed a bracing cup of her strongest blend. What was up with J.C.? Fiddling with the chips, she wished someone or something would fill the yawning void of silence.

"Eat your sandwich," J.C. instructed.

Maddie's head whipped up, but she saw that he was speaking to Chrissy who had taken only one bite.

"I'm not hungry," she complained.

"Probably because we forgot to bless the food," Maddie blurted, needing the prayer that began all her meals. Needing the Lord's guidance to get her through this unknown minefield. "J.C.?"

Hesitating only a few moments, he set his sandwich on the table, then clasped his hands together. "Dear Lord, please let us be thankful for this nourishment. May it strengthen us in all ways and fortify our resolve. In the name of your son. Amen."

"Amen," Maddie echoed.

But Chrissy didn't join in. Maddie wondered if the child had been counseled by their pastor, if she was receiving the comfort of fellowship. Her own connection to the Lord was what had gotten Maddie through losing her father. She missed going to church. After Lillian's first stroke, Maddie had tried to continue taking her to worship services. But Lillian's attention wandered and often she forgot why they were there, speaking aloud during the sermon or prayers. The pastor visited weekly, but it wasn't the same as being part of the loving body of worshippers.

J.C.'s cell phone rang, sounding especially loud. "Hello." He listened for a few moments. "Right here." He handed the phone to Maddie.

"Hello?" She heard Sam's voice and felt some of her tension dissipate. "Is Mom okay?" Listening to Sam's assurances, she sneaked a glance at J.C. and realized he was listening. Sam offered to keep Lillian entertained as long as needed. "You're sure? Okay, then. We'll be ready for her by evening."

"She's going to be gone *all* day?" Chrissy questioned.

"Well, until things are a little more settled."

"You expect to get everything settled by tonight?" J.C. quizzed. The words were tame enough, but the undertones in his voice were anything but ordinary.

What was he getting at? It seemed the walls of

the large apartment were shrinking, boxing her in. Swallowing, Maddie wished she could set time back. Back before they had found the fireplace. Back before the kindness in his eyes had turned to distrust.

Chapter Nine

Maddie worked like a madwoman to get every last knickknack in order. Lillian was fine with the new apartment, for the most part not realizing she was in a different place. She wondered at the elevator every time they used it, but that, too, was forgotten quickly.

Once Lillian had gotten to the apartment on moving day, Chrissy seemed to relax. Maddie knew the child felt that everything she had or wanted was always taken away, so Lillian's reappearance was an apparent comfort. While the duo played checkers or rearranged the large dollhouse that had been Maddie's as a child, she was able to concentrate on final details in the shop. Her grand opening was set for Friday and Saturday. Not that she expected it to be all that grand, but it was the official kickoff.

In choosing the days, she wanted stay-at-home moms to be able to stop by on Friday because many of them spent Saturdays with their husbands. For people who enjoyed coming downtown on Saturdays, she hoped her new sandwich-style advertising board that sat on the sidewalk would entice the crowd. The fair weather held and she placed inviting tables outside beneath the aged elms that lined Main Street.

By Friday, Maddie felt like a child on Christmas morning. Would people respond to this different sort of shop? Had she gone overboard on the old-world café look? Did people in Rosewood even drink tea? The sandwiches would be made to order, but she'd baked long into the night to prepare the pastries, petits fours and tiny cakes. Now, she looked at them as though alien invaders filled the glass-fronted display case. What had she been thinking? What man would want one of the delicate little jam tarts? Or mincemeat tartlets? She pictured large manly hands trying to grasp them and decided the whole idea was insanity.

Brewing fresh coffee for non-tea drinkers, she set out small pitchers of rich cream as well as vintage salt cellars filled with sugar. A curiosity, that's what her shop would be. People would shake their heads at the *Carter Folly*.

"Are you open yet?" Emma McAllister asked. Smiling, she held the hands of her two youngest children. "I'm so glad you picked a weekday for the launch."

"Yes, yes, of course." Maddie ran her hands down the sides of her apron, willing them to be still. "You can sit anywhere you want. I have a few child-size tables next to the adult ones in that corner." She pointed. "In case the kids would like to have their own little table."

"Perfect. A few friends are going to meet me and I'd love a grown-up table."

Soon Emma's *few* friends crowded the shop, oohing and aahing over the sweets in the display case, then ordering some of everything. Almost all of them also purchased tea blends to take home.

From her nook, Lillian visited with more people than she had seen in years. She couldn't remember names, but she enjoyed the interaction. People dropped in all day, even in what Maddie had expected to be the lull time. Chrissy popped in after school and promptly claimed her spot beside Lillian, engrossed in all the activity.

By five-thirty, when Maddie turned the Open sign to Closed, she was joyfully exhausted. "Can you believe the turnout?"

Lillian nodded vigorously. "I always said you ought to open your shop."

Maddie kissed her mother's delicate cheek. "And you were right."

"Will it be this busy all the time?" Chrissy asked.

"Probably not," Maddie answered realistically. "It's a novelty right now, but that's okay. I never expected to have steady traffic like the café does." The local dining spot was open before dawn and stayed open until well after the dinner hour. But the café had a small staff, not a sole proprietor. Those hours weren't feasible for either her type of business or life. Lillian needed a relatively early dinner because she went to bed soon after. And Maddie wasn't going to neglect her mother in favor of the Tea Cart. "Chrissy, I bet with all the commotion, you didn't get to your homework."

"We did numbers," Chrissy mumbled.

Numbers? Looking closer, Maddie saw a completed math homework sheet.

"Mrs. Lillian helped," Chrissy admitted.

Her mother had always been a whiz at math. Funny how she could remember to calculate but didn't have a clue what she'd eaten for breakfast. "That's great. I didn't want the opening to interfere with your schoolwork." Chrissy's performance at school had improved slightly but was nowhere near the straight A's she used to bring home.

"Are we going to have cake for dinner?" Chrissy asked.

Laughing, Maddie shook her head. Delighted that the child had any interest in eating, she smiled. "Knowing today would be crazy, I made lasagna. Just have to warm it up."

"Uncle James isn't home yet."

Being the city's sole neurologist, J.C.'s hours weren't predictable. He could come home promptly at six or in the wee hours of the night. "Lasagna reheats well."

"A lot of times it's better the second time around," Lillian commented.

"Why don't we go upstairs, get things going? I'll stick the lasagna in the oven. We can pick out a DVD to watch or a game to play."

Chrissy fetched Lillian's wheelchair from where it was stashed nearby. The child was becoming territorial about Lillian, which pleased Maddie. Maybe it was the transition Chrissy needed to accept supervisory adults other than her parents. J.C. and Maddie had offered countless times to help Chrissy with her homework and she always refused; yet today she had allowed Lillian to help. Apparently she didn't view Lillian as a threat, someone who would take her mother's place. Each step, no matter how minuscule, was a step. Although Chrissy might not realize it, Maddie knew the Lord was watching over her. His plan had given them all renewed hope.

While Chrissy pushed Lillian's chair toward the elevator, Maddie's gaze strayed out the window onto Main Street. J.C. wasn't anywhere in sight. Remembering his strained behavior the past few weeks, she wondered if the same was true of him. Was he feeling hope? Or regret? Regret for allowing her this much access in his life?

"Are you coming?" Chrissy called out.

"You go ahead. I have to put some things away, but I'll be up in a few minutes." However, after the elevator doors closed, Maddie didn't move, instead holding a dishcloth as she stared outside. And hated the lump forming in the pit of her stomach.

J.C. had debated staying late at the office, catching up on notes, but he knew it was a delaying tactic that wasn't fair to Chrissy. He'd barely seen her for five minutes early that morning. The entire building had been in a mild frenzy as the Tea Cart prepared for the big launch. He could have stolen a few minutes to stop by, but he'd chosen to extend his hospital rounds.

Stepping inside the shop, J.C. saw that Maddie had left two lamps aglow on each side of the main room, just enough to softly illuminate the tidy area. The light above the stairwell was also left on. For him?

Knowing he couldn't delay any longer, J.C. mounted the steps. The door to the Carters' apartment was ajar. Reaching his own, he saw a note tacked near eye level. *Lasagna for dinner. Chrissy's with us. Maddie*

He pushed open the door. The last specks of light from the sunset had faded. And the apartment was dark. Suiting his mood, J.C. didn't turn on a lamp. Enough light from the corridor spilled inside so that he could see the furniture. Dropping his briefcase on a chair, he shrugged out of his jacket, loosened his tie and pulled it off.

Voices from the other apartment drifted toward him, small snatches of conversation, a little laughter. Feeling too much like a sulky schoolboy, J.C. forced himself to cross the hall. In a glance, he could see the table was set for four. Looked like they hadn't eaten yet.

Maddie spotted him first. Although smiling, she looked hesitant. Chrissy and Lillian were engaged in what appeared to be an intense checkers match.

"No moves left!" Chrissy announced triumphantly. She glanced up just then, noticed him and quieted.

He couldn't allow his reservations about Maddie to affect how he treated his niece. "You still the all-time checkers champ?"

A small smile emerged.

"I hope you're hungry," Maddie added. "Not that the menu's a surprise. I put that in the note. We have salad and garlic bread, too."

J.C. wondered why she sounded so nervous. "So how'd the grand opening go?"

"Good. Lots of people. Of course there won't be that many people every day. The shop's a novelty right now. And I'm not sure the menu's male-friendly. Little sandwiches, little desserts, little..." She swallowed. "Little stuff...you know."

She didn't usually prattle like this. He glanced across the room. "Did everybody cope well?"

"Mother enjoyed all the company and Chrissy fit right in. That was after school, of course. Because today's Friday and she had school. She won't tomorrow because it'll be Saturday and..."

J.C. looked back at Maddie. "Something wrong?"

"No, no. What would be wrong?" She gripped her apron as though she expected hurricane-strength winds to tear it away.

"Good."

"Dinner's ready. We kept it warm—the lasagna, I mean. Warm salad wouldn't taste good unless it was German potato salad or maybe a wilted salad that's supposed to be warm. Oh, and the garlic bread, it's warm."

Because Maddie looked ready to burst out of her own skin, he nodded. "You all could have eaten without me."

She waved toward the pristine china on the table. "No bother."

Looked like she'd gone to enough trouble, especially after the adrenaline-draining day. She had to be tired. "You cooked. I'll clean up."

"But—"

"Let's eat first, argue later."

"We don't have to argue—"

"Did you say something about lasagna?"

"Oh! Yes. It's vegetarian. Mom? Chrissy? Dinner's ready." She glanced at J.C. "I'll just grab the salad and pitcher of tea."

When Chrissy was in hearing distance, he leaned close, whispering. "What's up with Maddie?"

Chrissy shrugged, her usual helpful self.

Wouldn't do any good to question Lillian since she couldn't remember the day.

He gestured to Chrissy. "Let's wash our hands."

She rolled her eyes but complied. Once his own hands were clean, too, they rejoined the others. Maddie fussed over the table settings, repositioning the serving dishes.

After he recited the blessing over their meal, J.C. accepted a hefty portion of the fragrant lasagna. "So, how many people did you have at the shop today?"

Maddie dropped the offset spatula she was using to serve the main dish. Recovering, she dabbed at the sauce that had spilled on the yellow tablecloth. "I don't know exactly. Emma McAllister was the first customer. Sam was next. She wanted to be the very first one, but Emma got here a little before the actual opening time. Of course the door was unlocked and it wasn't a big deal that she came early." Maddie finally paused to breathe. "And she brought the twins. They sat at one of the kid-size tables."

J.C. began to wonder if she'd swallowed a tape recorder that she couldn't turn off. "Was business steady then?"

"All day. It was amazing. I kept waiting for the lull." This time when Maddie paused, she seemed to actually collect her thoughts before she resumed speaking. "It's a novelty for Rosewood."

"And it fills a niche. The town's never had an eatery that's targeted for women. Café's good, but not all feminine."

She frowned. "So the men won't like the Tea Cart at all?"

"Didn't say that. But you told me yourself that more women tend to frequent tea shops. It's not easy to find a new target market these days. Everything's saturated. You came up with something new for the town."

Her cheeks flushed a light pink. "I suppose it's hard to believe it's really happening. I dreamed about opening this shop for so long…" Maddie reached over, covering Lillian's hand. "Mom always believed it would work."

Lillian smiled but she looked tired. "Maddie can do anything she sets her mind to."

"Did you get a nap today?" J.C. questioned.

When Lillian looked blank, Maddie answered for her. "No. And she's usually in bed about now."

He frowned. "You shouldn't have waited dinner on me."

Chastened, Maddie looked down. "I just thought…" She cleared her throat. "You're right, of course. I was only thinking of myself."

Feeling as though he had kicked a puppy, J.C. laid his fork down. "I didn't mean that."

Maddie's lips trembled slightly before she firmed them together in a grim line. "I need to keep my priorities in order. Mom is my top priority." She looked down at her own untouched plate. "You should eat the lasagna while it's hot."

Noticing that Chrissy was staring at him, J.C. picked up his fork. "This is good, isn't it, Chrissy?"

"You haven't tasted it yet," she pointed out.

Wincing inside, he loaded his fork. "Dig in."

While he chewed, Chrissy picked at her food, finally edging a little bit of lasagna on her fork.

"It's really good," J.C. declared.

Maddie kept her gaze on her own plate.

Feeling even worse, J.C. searched for something, anything to say. "You'll probably have an even bigger turnout tomorrow."

Maddie blanched, then looked at Lillian.

J.C. belatedly realized he had said exactly the wrong thing. "I'll be around tomorrow so Lillian and I can hang out while you're in the shop."

Still looking wounded, Maddie stared at him.

"What do you say, Lillian?" he asked.

"I'm tired, Maddie."

Looking even more guilty, Maddie pushed her chair back. "Come on, Mom. Let's get you ready for bed. I'll bring in a cup of warm milk."

Lillian's shoulders drooped as Maddie led her away.

"Jiminy…" Chrissy muttered.

"What?"

"You don't know?" she questioned, wide-eyed.

J.C. knew all right. He had managed to ruin the celebratory dinner. Not to mention causing Maddie to feel as though she had neglected her mother. He just hated that his nine-year-old niece had figured it out before he had.

* * *

The following morning, the shop was packed within fifteen minutes after opening time. It seemed that all of Rosewood had turned out to see the newest business on Main Street. A quirk, Maddie kept telling herself. Even when Samantha stepped behind the counter and pulled on an apron so she could help. Between them, they could barely keep up with all the orders. Lillian came down for a while, then J.C. took her back upstairs. Still feeling like the worst kind of daughter, Maddie fretted about Lillian until Samantha popped upstairs to check on her.

"She's fine," Sam reported. "Watching a little TV, drifting off."

"Does she look tired?"

"Maddie, stop it. So, one day out of how many? Thousands? You focused more on yourself than your mother and she got tired. That is in no way a terrible thing. Not to mention, if J.C. had gotten back from work sooner, dinner wouldn't have been so late. I think I need to have a talk with him and—"

"No! That'll just make things worse."

"This arrangement is supposed to help all of you, not just him. Did you complain when you kept Chrissy overnight because he had to go to the hospital? No. It won't hurt him to help out."

Exasperated, Maddie stared at her friend. "Do I have to remind you who funded this shop? Who's letting us live here for free?"

Samantha grumbled beneath her breath, then solidly met Maddie's gaze. "Fine. He did a good thing, but you can't feel indebted forever."

"Business probably won't be this steady after the newness wears off anyway."

"So now you're hoping your business fails?"

"No, I just need to clone myself."

"Or hire someone to help when you can afford it. Meanwhile, I'll volunteer."

"You can't do that."

"Want to try and stop me?" Samantha retorted.

"I've already imposed too much. You've watched Mom a lot lately."

"I wouldn't have made it when I came back to Rosewood if the whole town hadn't pitched in and helped, you included. Let me give back, just a little."

Maddie guessed she would never be able to convince her friend otherwise. "Not too much, though, okay?"

Samantha grinned. "I'm not punching a time clock."

"Yes, but—"

"Maddie!" Sam grabbed her arm, her grin gone. "Look."

Owen stalked toward her as though he owned the shop.

"Will you watch the counter?"

"Yes, and if you need backup, holler." Sam lifted her cane as though it was a sword.

"That *probably* won't be necessary." Maddie stepped from behind the counter, suddenly feeling vulnerable, uncomfortable in her own place. Realizing that, she straightened her shoulders.

Without asking, Owen took her elbow, steering her toward the door.

Maddie tried to shake off his grasp, but he tightened it further. Not wanting to cause a scene, she waited until they were outside on the sidewalk. Yanking her arm away, she glared at him. "What do you think you're doing?"

"Better question. What do *you* think you're doing?"

Bewildered, she gaped. "What are you talking about?"

"You couldn't marry me because your mother was your first concern. Forget that we were engaged, planning a wedding. You called everything off because of her."

She blinked. "Why are you bringing all this up now? It's ancient history."

He flung his arm in the direction of the shop, then stood far too close, his face in hers. "Really? What do you call this?"

Jerking her head back, she retreated, needing more space between them. "It's my tea shop."

"Exactly!" Triumph filled his voice. "The one you couldn't open because of your mother."

"So?"

"What's wrong with you?" he demanded, his voice gritty.

Appalled, she wondered what was wrong with him. A week ago he'd tried to talk to her again and she had escaped when his cell phone rang. Fortunately, she thought to lock the front door so he couldn't follow. He had knocked, then rattled the doorknob, finally leaving. She had thought it would be the last of him.

"If you can open a shop, you can get married!"

"Owen, it's been years. You didn't even try to keep in touch." She didn't remind him that he was the one who issued the ultimatum.

"Because you insisted your mother was more important." The way his voice curled when he said *mother* made it sound like an ugly word. "Clearly that's not true."

Still confused, she wasn't sure what he wanted to hear. "If you want to be friends—"

"Friends?" he snarled.

Maddie took another step backward. "Then what?"

Reaching into his pocket, he pulled out a ring, the two-carat, emerald-shaped diamond she had returned to him.

She shook her head. "Surely you've moved on?"

"Don't you have that backward?" Again, he flung his arm toward the shop. "You're the one moving on."

"Owen, I don't know what this is about, but I'm in the middle of my grand opening." She turned away from him.

"This isn't over." The anger in his voice made his words sound like a threat.

A chill traveled up her spine. Irritated, she shook

her head, dismissing him. She whipped open the door, but refused to give him the satisfaction of running inside.

"What did he want?" Samantha demanded, in full mother bear mode.

"I'm not really sure. Apparently he's still mad because I've opened my own business."

"It doesn't have anything to do with him!"

"You and I know that, but I'm not sure Owen's playing with a full deck. He's acting as though our engagement was on hold all this time."

Frowning, Samantha looked out through the front window. "That's kind of scary."

"No, sad maybe."

"I don't know…"

"Probably just a power thing, Sam. What's really sad is that I didn't see one atom of the man I used to know."

"Just be glad he's out of your life."

Maddie glanced out the bay window. She hoped Sam was right.

Chapter Ten

❦

Spring in Rosewood elicited fields of wildflowers at the outskirts of town and the blooming of multihued azaleas in nearly every garden in town. Sudden downpours of rain could trigger flash floods in the arroyos, but sunshine filled Sunday's sky.

Lillian's new medications were working pretty well, enough so that Maddie decided it was time to try taking her mother to church again. J.C.'s schedule was clear and he offered to drive. His SUV was more suited to carrying four adults and a wheelchair than her small Honda.

When they arrived, Chrissy dragged her feet, dawdling as they walked into the Sunday school building. Maddie placed a worn, familiar Bible in her mother's lap. It was one thing Lillian had never forgotten. Maddie decided to stay with her mother in the older ladies' class. If she coped well, Maddie hoped Lillian could interact with the other members. As the hour passed, Lillian's attention wandered, but she was content.

Afterward, Lillian chatted with the ladies as they strolled toward the sanctuary. A few lingered, matching their pace to the wheelchair. Hoping her mother wouldn't tire, Maddie found places at the end of a pew close to the back, then folded the wheelchair so that she could lean it out of the way. But she wanted it close in case they needed a quick escape. Lillian could still forget where she was and talk out loud, interrupting the service.

Maddie soon forgot her worry, distracted when person after person came to greet them and comment on the new shop.

"We knew it was going to be a smashing success." Samantha beamed, winking at Maddie.

Emma McAllister was only a few feet behind. "It really is super, Maddie, and we've never had anything like it here in Rosewood."

Which is what J.C. had said.

Chrissy slipped into the pew, crossing past Maddie to sit beside Lillian. J.C. was right behind her. Not expecting him to climb over two adults, Maddie asked the others to scoot down. They did but didn't leave as much space as Maddie would have liked. When J.C. sat beside her, his arm pressed into hers. At first she couldn't tell if the warmth that swamped her was coming from him or from the flush she felt.

Holding herself rigid, she didn't move when he

reached for a hymnal, brushing against her, then settling back in place. Belatedly, she realized she could stop holding her breath. Feeling ridiculous, she lectured herself. *They were in church. He just happened to be sitting next to her. Just like any other member of the congregation.*

But he wasn't just any other member. He was her business partner, landlord, the man who caused her pulse to quicken, her thoughts to meander toward romance. Initially worried that Lillian might not make it through the morning service, now Maddie wondered if she would.

Bowing their heads for the opening prayer, Maddie added urgent, silent words, asking the Lord to help her through this hour, to calm her racing feelings. Both the piano and organ played the prelude to the first hymn. As they stood, J.C. offered his hymnal to share. Maddie started to refuse, planning to use her mother as an excuse, but Chrissy had already opened another hymnal and was sharing it with Lillian.

J.C.'s voice was a pleasing surprise. Hitting each note evenly, he sang the words with ease. She wondered why he wasn't in the choir. The thought melded into another, remembering the timbre of his voice when they had crashed into the fireplace. The way it had caused her skin to prickle, to raise her awareness of him.

Abruptly, she tried to step backward. The pew already hugged the back of her knees and she swayed. J.C. immediately caught her arm, holding it until the song finished. Flushing even deeper, Maddie swallowed, wondering how much more embarrassed she could become.

Thankfully, she sank back onto the pew, momentarily forgetting that J.C. was still pressed next to her. Although she had always been able to lose herself in the sermon, today she scarcely heard the pastor's words. She certainly didn't absorb any of them. Maddie tried to put a little space between them by inching toward her mother. Lillian smiled, then patted her knee affectionately, but she didn't budge. To make matters worse, she could see that J.C. was listening intently to the message, not affected as she was.

By the closing prayer, Maddie was ready to bolt out of the pew. She needed and wanted to listen to the sermon. Today had taught her that wouldn't happen unless she made sure she didn't sit by J.C. again. Feeling guilty as she shook the pastor's hand, Maddie silently promised the Lord to behave properly in the future.

Relieved to be away from the jarring sensations, she nearly screeched when J.C. suggested lunch. Her voice came out in a squeak. "I'm sure Mom is tired."

"Lunch?" Lillian responded gamely. "Where?"

Rosewood's café was closed on Sunday like the rest of the businesses.

"There's a new place on the highway," J.C. replied. "A big chain outfit, but they have a good menu."

Maddie tried to refuse.

But Lillian beat her to the punch. "That sounds lovely." She patted Chrissy's arm. "Would you like that?"

For once Chrissy didn't shrug her indifference. "Okay."

Great.

Maddie tried to maneuver in beside her mother. Lillian waved her away. "Let Chrissy sit with me."

J.C. stowed the wheelchair in the back and Maddie reluctantly slipped into the front seat.

After driving about fifteen miles, Maddie couldn't remain silent. "How far is this place?"

"Not too much farther." He glanced at her. "Do you have something else on for today?"

Her lips froze. Of course she didn't. And since he lived across the hall she couldn't avoid him. "Just wondered. I haven't seen this restaurant before."

"Chrissy likes their French fries and cheese sticks."

Even better. A place that served food that would go directly to her hips and stay there.

As J.C. had told her, they drove only a few more miles. The parking lot was packed.

"If we have to wait, I don't think Mom will have

the energy," Maddie told him in a low voice, not wanting to be trumped by her mother again.

"Their service is good. Why don't we check it out?"

Wishing she could will his vehicle to peel off in the opposite direction, she kept quiet as they parked. It didn't bode well that J.C. unloaded the wheelchair. Once Lillian was inside, she would no doubt want to stay.

The wait was only ten minutes, all of which Maddie spent plotting to make certain she didn't sit close to J.C.

The hostess led them to a small curved booth. "I'm sorry it's a bit on the small side. But a larger table won't open up for at least thirty minutes."

"It's fine," J.C. assured the young woman.

Maddie silently agreed, not wanting to lengthen their stay. She looked over the compact booth. Lillian needed to sit on the outside. Maddie assumed J.C. and Chrissy would slide into the middle section and she could take the remaining outer position.

"Lillian, why don't we get you seated first," he suggested.

She allowed him to assist her out of the wheelchair and into her spot.

Pleased, Maddie teetered on her heels.

"Chrissy, hop in this side," J.C. instructed.

She complied and Maddie suppressed her grin. However, unaccustomed to wearing her dress shoes, she tilted more than she expected. J.C.'s arm shot out to steady her. The next second he was ushering her into position between Chrissy and himself.

Maddie bent her head. *Why Lord?*

The hostess had remained and she placed menus in front of each of them. "Your server will be here in just a minute."

Maddie grabbed her menu, wanting to decide as quickly as possible so she could eat quickly, then leave quickly. Quickly, quickly, quickly. Yet her attention wandered when J.C. shifted, his long legs stretched out beneath the table and more important, next to her. She tried to scoot over.

"Ouch!" Chrissy complained.

"I'm sorry, just trying to get comfortable," she mumbled, feeling the warmth flooding her face, then grabbing a menu to hide behind.

"Lillian, they make a great chicken pot pie," J.C. suggested.

Lowering her menu slightly, Maddie saw the confusion in her mother's face. Guiltily, she realized she had been more concerned about herself than her mother. All the choices on the menu would be overwhelming for Lillian. "You like chicken pot pie," she encouraged.

"And you can have some of my fries," Chrissy offered.

That brought a smile to Lillian's face.

Watching her mother and Chrissy interacting, Maddie realized how fortunate she was. The Lord had answered her prayers for both assistance and guidance. Financially, they had a solid future. Before J.C.'s offer, she had worried constantly about how they would manage. And she was fulfilling her dream. The shop was a wonder. She couldn't ask for a better situation.

Keeping that thought in mind, she ate her lunch, tried to ignore the flutters J.C.'s proximity caused and made herself concentrate on the good. When they were ready to go home, she couldn't understand the jab of disappointment when J.C. left her side and stood up. Deciding she was more fickle than the storms in spring, Maddie made herself smile.

J.C. took charge of Lillian's wheelchair, Chrissy walking next to Lillian as they crossed the lobby. Maddie paused to pick up mints for each of them.

"Are you here with him?" Owen demanded from behind her.

She turned around, wishing she had seen Owen first so she could have avoided him. "I'm just on my way out."

J.C. glanced back, then turned the wheelchair around so all three of them were staring. Uncomfortable, she waved him on. "I'll meet you at the car." Waiting only until he complied, she lowered her voice. "As I said, I'm on my way out."

"You didn't answer me."

Exasperated, she clenched the mints in one fist. "It's none of your business."

"Of course it's my business!" Owen raised his voice and several people craned their heads to watch.

"You're making a scene."

"You think I care?"

"Apparently not. I'm sorry if you have some mixed-up idea about us, but you need to let it go."

"How can you say that?"

Perplexed, Maddie shook her head. "Owen, I don't know what's gotten into you, but please stop." Not listening to his retort, she fled outside.

Having stowed the wheelchair, J.C. settled Lillian in the backseat while Chrissy hopped in next to her without any coaching. J.C. helped Lillian buckle her seat belt. "Looks like we're all set."

"You're such a nice young man," Lillian told him. "Like Maddie's young man."

He froze.

"Who's that?" Chrissy asked.

"We just saw him," Lillian murmured. "His name is…" She shook her head. "Did you eat your dessert?"

J.C. recognized that Lillian was tired. It was possible that she was wrong about Owen Radley. Instantly, the image of Owen and Maddie on the sidewalk flashed in his thoughts.

Closing the backseat door, he spotted Maddie rushing toward the vehicle. By the time he skirted the hood to open her door, she hastily climbed inside, looking as though she was fleeing the scene of a crime.

The only conversation in the SUV was Chrissy's chattering to Lillian. J.C. pulled out of the parking lot back onto the highway. His mind racing, J.C. could rationalize Lillian's wanderings as simply fatigue. That didn't explain why he had seen Owen with Maddie before. Was he, as Lillian phrased it, Maddie's *young man?*

But as much as J.C. wanted to ask, he couldn't. Not only was it the wrong time and place with Chrissy and Lillian in the back, but Maddie also hadn't shared any more of her personal life with him. He knew who her closest friends were, but she had never divulged information about any romantic interests. Was that why she had pulled back from him so abruptly when they discovered the fireplace?

Silent until they were close to the outskirts of town, Maddie finally spoke. "Thank you for lunch."

He glanced at her. "It's an interesting place."

She avoided his gaze. "Yes."

Tell me what Owen means to you. The words nearly tumbled out, but he clamped his lips shut.

Chrissy piped up from behind. "I wish the drugstore was open so we could get shakes."

Distracted, he looked in the rearview mirror. "You just ate dessert." Then it hit him. He wasn't having to coerce her into eating.

"I could make shakes," Maddie offered. "We have chocolate ice cream."

Chrissy's favorite. He hadn't noticed that Maddie was getting to know his niece so well. It reinforced his need to know what else he had missed.

Chapter Eleven

The following weeks encouraged Maddie to believe her tea shop could succeed. Not expecting the same volume of business as her grand opening weekend, she had been pleasantly surprised to see that many of the people, primarily women, became repeat customers.

"It's *the* place for ladies' lunches," Samantha assured her.

Maddie had added muffins and cookies from the local bakery to the display case. She had planned on making everything herself, but preparing the tarts, pastries, sandwich fillings and other items on her menu took quite a bit of time. And Lillian still required the same amount of care.

Glancing over to the nook where Lillian chatted with one of the women from her Sunday school class, Maddie silently prayed that her mother would continue to flourish in their new environment.

"She's loving it," Samantha commented, breaking off a bite of a coconut macaroon.

"I've been so blessed."

"You deserve it."

Maddie shook her head.

Samantha tapped her cane. "I'm pretty well versed in the blessings area, you know."

Her friend's recovery had been nothing short of a miracle. When Sam had returned to Rosewood, she had been paralyzed with no hope of recovery. Prayer, determination and J.C.'s expertise had defied that diagnosis. "Yeah, I know."

"So how *is* J.C. these days?"

"Subtle, Sam, real subtle."

"And you're avoiding the issue."

Maddie shrugged.

"Now you're acting like Chrissy. Give."

Chuckling, Maddie picked up the tray of tarts, rearranging the ones that were left. "Sorry to disappoint you, but there's nothing to tell."

"Why don't I believe that?"

"Because you're a hopeless romantic. This time, though, your radar's off." She glanced again at Lillian's nook. Chrissy sat beside her, concentrating on her new project.

"What's Chrissy doing over there?"

"She's making name tags for Mom's friends so she can know who she's speaking to when they come in. See that basket? We're going to keep them in it on the little table by the door."

"Wouldn't it be easier to write them out when people drop by?"

"Oh, these are permanent name tags. Chrissy decided they ought to look like little teapots. So I helped her with the mold, bought the clay, paints and pin backs. And she's making and painting each one."

"Clever."

Maddie frowned. "She's a bright girl."

"Then why don't you look pleased?"

"She's still not doing as well as she should in school."

"I'm guessing that's natural," Sam protested. "I can't imagine how she's coped."

"And she resents anyone who wants to take her parents' places. J.C. said she ran off every nanny, housekeeper and babysitter he ever hired."

Sam looked pointedly at Lillian. "She seems content when she's with your mother."

"I know." Their bond kept increasing and the relationship was helping both of them.

"It's going to take time...bringing your family together."

Knowing that would never truly happen brought a piercing pain. Although Lillian could fulfill the spot of a missing grandparent, Maddie couldn't do the same in a motherly capacity. It wouldn't be fair. When J.C. married, his wife would be the one to step into that role. Watching how earnestly Chrissy was working on the name tags brought a lump to her throat. The child was encroaching on her heart, as well.

Along with her uncle.

Samantha poured a fresh cup of tea. "Let's be grateful for today's blessings. The other will come along in time."

Knowing Sam had read her thoughts, Maddie swallowed. "You're right. The Lord has always watched over us." And even if she wasn't part of Chrissy's future, she could enjoy each and every day with the child while she prepared her own heart for a life without her new family.

By Sunday, J.C. was eager to attend worship service. His mind had been in such confusion that he needed the fellowship, as well as the guidance in the pastor's words. Regardless of where he was, what he was doing, Maddie kept popping into his thoughts. Knowing he should be concentrating on Chrissy's happiness, J.C. wanted to reinforce his commitment and keep the Lord close.

Pulling on his suit jacket, he smelled pancakes from across the hall. Chrissy had gone over while he showered and dressed. They had fallen into a routine of eating with Maddie and Lillian. The only thing he could really cook involved meat and an outdoor grill.

After school each day, Chrissy walked home, spending the afternoons in the Tea Cart. Then she headed upstairs with Maddie and Lillian. If he couldn't leave the office or hospital, they ate dinner without him. Either way, Chrissy was never left on her own any longer. It was an overpowering sense of relief. One that should have made him content. Instead, his thoughts were continually spinning around Maddie and Owen.

The door to the Carters' apartment was ajar as it usually was once the building was locked up for the night and on Sundays. Ever since Owen's intrusion, J.C. made sure they were safely locked in when the shop wasn't open.

Maddie stood at the stove flipping pancakes on the griddle while maple sausage sizzled in a second pan. Must be tasty. Chrissy's plate was nearly empty.

J.C. pulled out a chair, sat down and reached for a napkin. "You better get dressed, Chrissy."

"Uh-uh."

He glanced at his watch. "We don't want to be late."

"I'm not going."

J.C. smoothed the napkin in his lap. "What do you mean?"

"That I'm *not* going," she said slowly, drawing out each word.

"Quit joking around and get dressed."

"You never listen to me," she replied, her lower lip wobbling a tiny bit.

"Of course I listen to you." Baffled, he studied his niece.

"Uh-uh. And I'm not going!" Shoving back her chair, she ran out and across the hall, slamming the front door of their apartment behind her.

Sobered, he glanced at Maddie. She had abandoned the cooking, frozen in place, holding a spatula in one hand as she stared out into the hall after Chrissy.

"She's not happy," Lillian commented. "Someone should talk to her."

J.C. knew who that somebody was. Pushing back his chair, he met Maddie's concerned gaze. She and Lillian remained silent as he left them.

Back in his own apartment, he saw immediately that Chrissy's bedroom door was closed. He knocked softly, but she didn't reply. "I'm coming in," he said in a voice loud enough to carry through the thick door.

Curled in the window seat, Chrissy's arms were crossed in silent defiance. It certainly wasn't the first time she had displayed defiance, but this time he suspected it ran far deeper.

"Pinker Belle," he began, using the nickname he'd coined when she was a baby. He remembered how tiny she had been. Her face pink and crinkling into early smiles, she'd made everyone around her happy since her first day on earth. Funny, he hadn't planned to call her that…hadn't used the moniker since her parents' deaths. For at least the hundredth time he longed for his sister's wisdom. "Want to tell me what this is about?"

"I told you." Her lip wobbled a bit more.

"Your mom and dad loved going to church. I always thought you did, too."

"It's different."

He knew in an instant what she meant.

"God didn't have to kill them," she continued, her voice warbling.

J.C. winced. "The Lord didn't kill them."

"He let them die!" she accused.

Differentiating wouldn't help. "The Lord gave them both life, you, as well. We don't always understand what happens to us, but He loves us, wants the best for us."

"Is the best letting Mommy and Daddy die?" Her lips no longer just wobbled. A wail erupted that broke his heart.

Immediately J.C. pulled her close, patting her back, trying to comfort her. "It's difficult for grownups to understand." He remembered the anguish when his own parents had died. "It's especially hard when you're young."

"That's no reason," she sobbed.

Knowing how keenly he felt the loss of his sister, he was all that more aware of Chrissy's pain. He let her cry until the final hiccuping sob was gone and the last of her tears trickled away. She pulled away, then stared out the window.

"Do you remember when your dad wanted to take off the training wheels on your bike?"

She didn't reply.

"You hated the idea…it was scary. He told you that you had to give it a try. If you really didn't like having them off, he would put them back on for you."

She scowled. "This isn't the same."

"The idea is. I want you to attend church while you search for the answers."

"And if I don't like it, I don't have to go back?"

That wasn't a promise he could make. "We will talk it over again."

She balked. "That's not fair."

He tucked a lock of unruly hair behind one ear. "Chrissy, you want to do what would make your parents happy, don't you?"

Reluctantly she nodded.

"Going to church would make them happy. They believed very strongly that God was in everything we see and touch, from leaves on a tree to puppies to the bluebonnets every spring."

Chrissy took a ragged breath, her red-rimmed eyes puffy from all the crying.

Considering how upset she was, he offered a compromise for the day. "Why don't we go see some of those things today? I'll pack a picnic basket and we'll worship under the sky God created."

"With Mrs. Lillian?" she questioned.

"I can ask. Next Sunday, we'll go to services at church. Now, go wash your face."

J.C. explained the situation to the Carters and

they were in instant agreement. Maddie offered to make the lunch. He drafted Chrissy to help gather blankets and lawn chairs so that she would have something useful to do that would distract her.

It took a little time for Maddie to make lunch because her sandwich fillings were all gone from the day before. She had to help Lillian change out of her Sunday dress into a knit blouse and corduroy jumper, then change her own clothes.

But in plenty of time for lunch, J.C. drove out of Rosewood to a perfect picnic area. The town park would have been fine, but J.C. wanted to put Chrissy right in the middle of nature. The glory of His work was always compelling.

As spring gradually advanced toward summer, the days were bright with sunshine and cloudless skies. Buds dotted the flowering trees and the withered grasses of summer were ripe with new shoots, coloring the fields.

Maddie helped him stretch out the hand-tied quilt beneath a canopy of newly sprouted leaves. She turned to glance at Lillian and Chrissy who were sitting side by side watching for white-tailed deer, wild turkeys or jackrabbits to run by on the brush-covered sloping hills.

J.C. saw the concern in Maddie's eyes. He hated to add to the worry she always carried for her mother, but he needed her help.

She set the picnic basket on one end of the quilt.

"I'm guessing no one's ready for lunch yet." Some of them had eaten a hearty breakfast not that long ago.

J.C. held the other two lawn chairs, not quite ready to set them up. "I'm worried that Chrissy isn't going to be easily convinced about going back to church."

Maddie's gaze swerved again toward Chrissy. "You can see so much of your sister and brother-in-law in her."

Surprised, he drew his eyebrows together. "I didn't know you met them."

"I didn't. I've been in their house, which gave me a look into their personalities. But it's mostly through Chrissy. Even though she hasn't stopped acting out, she's thoughtful, considerate. How many nine-year-olds would choose to spend their time with an older woman who has a failing mind? And Chrissy never loses her patience. If Mom rambles, Chrissy just listens." Maddie smiled as Lillian offered Chrissy a butterscotch Life Saver. "Even though Chrissy prefers cherry candy, she always picks out butterscotch when we go to the store because she knows Mom likes it." Maddie lifted her gaze to meet his eyes. "Your sister was like that, wasn't she?"

Exactly like that. For a moment it seemed as though Fran stood at his side, her voice soft. *She understands you, little brother. Don't let her go.*

"I hope I haven't upset you," Maddie continued, her eyes darkening to a grassy green.

"They do change," he muttered, fascinated by her eyes, the delicate blush of her cheeks, the way she pursed her lips when concentrating.

"Excuse me?"

"Yes, Fran was like that."

"So, what are we going to do?" she asked quietly.

It wasn't a presumption, it was who Maddie was. Despite caring for her mother and running a brand-new business, he suspected it hadn't even occurred to Maddie that Chrissy wasn't her problem. "I told Chrissy she could see the Lord in everything around her. If she keeps seeing His wonders..."

"She can believe again," Maddie finished the thought for him.

"That's what did it for me," he confided, thinking of his ex-wife's betrayal, how his faith had faltered.

Questions filled Maddie's remarkable eyes, but she didn't ask.

"It was a while ago," he explained, not wanting to spill the ugly details. Trust wasn't all he had lost. He was ashamed of what had happened, the fact that Amy had tossed away their marriage as though it had been the kitchen trash.

She seemed to understand his reluctance. "We've all had trials that test our faith..."

"Look!" Chrissy exclaimed loudly. "A deer."

Realizing he had walked closer to Maddie than he

had meant to, J.C. stepped back. The breeze stirred between them as though missing the near contact.

The expression on Maddie's face seemed to resonate his own thoughts. *Surely not.*

"Did you see?" Chrissy asked. "Maddie? Uncle James?"

"Missed that one." He cleared his throat. "Find me another."

"Uncle James!" Chrissy harrumphed but turned back to scrutinize the hills.

J.C. carried the last two lawn chairs away from the tree, plunking one down beside Lillian, the other by Chrissy. He rationalized that he should spend this time with his niece, not that he needed to put distance between himself and Maddie. This wasn't the time to get lost in his own longings. Yes, J.C. reminded himself, Chrissy needed all of his attention.

Yet when Maddie lifted her face to watch for deer, he studied her profile rather than his surroundings. A rabbit would have to jump in his lap before he'd see it. She was pretty, but he'd known that since their first meeting. It was something more, something he didn't have the courage to explore. Love with all its tricky complications had died for him after his divorce. Anyone with his track record would have to agree. Sure, he used to dream about the one perfect woman he could grow old with. But once the eyes dimmed and the skin lost its youthful freshness, what was left of that woman? Was her heart bigger than the sky? Were her morals higher than the Rockies? And her spirit? Her faith?

As he watched, Maddie entwined her hand with her mother's, giving an encouraging squeeze.

"It's beautiful out here, isn't it, Mom?"

Lillian looked over the budding field, the spring grasses stirring faintly. "Soon the bluebonnets will be gone."

"We can enjoy them now."

Content, Lillian leaned back, settling into the chair.

As J.C. watched, he wondered. And wished it was his hand Maddie held.

Chrissy's birthday was approaching. And she had to decide whether she wanted a party at the Tea Cart or an outdoor gathering. Maddie and J.C. had been taking her on hikes and nature walks for weeks now. Chrissy reluctantly kept her part of the deal and didn't balk at going to church. But she was still a work in progress.

Maddie felt she was, too. Owen continued to annoy her every chance he got, and J.C. continued to ignore her. Well, maybe not ignore, but he didn't interact the way he had. Apparently, she didn't need to worry about her own weakness since he didn't show a shred of interest. Relieved, that's what she should be. Relieved.

Then why was she so disappointed?

Maddie sighed as she wiped off the shop counter.

"Something wrong, dear?" Lillian asked.

"No, of course not." Maddie turned to Chrissy. "Are you leaning one way or the other about your party?"

Chrissy climbed down from Lillian's side and circled around the smaller tables. "Will everybody fit in here?"

"Let's see. There are eighteen kids in your class."

"If we have hot dogs, too, I could invite the boys. They might not come if they think it's a tea party for just girls. And Lexi's brother, Chance, won't come if he's the only boy."

"Good point," Maddie agreed, holding up her fingers to count. "Your uncle, Mom…"

"Lexi and Chance," Chrissy reminded her.

Maddie tapped her two next fingers to include them. "Everyone should fit just fine. And because it's your party, we'll have an extra special menu, all your favorites and whatever little boys will eat."

"Uncle James used to be a boy."

Lillian snickered.

Maddie coughed so she wouldn't laugh, as well. "Then we'll ask him."

"Hot dogs. Definitely hot dogs," James decided. "Pizza's good, too."

"Pizza?" Chrissy's voice quickened in excitement. It would be a special treat because Rosewood didn't have a pizza parlor. "I could make pizzas,"

Maddie offered. "I'm guessing cheese and pepperoni would be the most popular."

"I like cheese," Chrissy announced.

"And I like pepperoni," J.C. added the male vote.

"Cheese pizza and pepperoni pizza. Hot dogs, of course. And your favorite cake—one layer chocolate, one layer vanilla."

"With your special frosting," Chrissy chirped.

"Both flavors?" Maddie questioned.

"Uh-huh." Chrissy reached for a dinner roll.

J.C.'s fork paused midair. "Both?"

"It's all butter cream," Maddie explained, "vanilla and chocolate."

Planning parties and menus wasn't his thing. "There'll be enough room for all the kids on a busy Saturday?"

"It'll work best if we plan for an afternoon party. The busiest time is from brunch until the early afternoon."

J.C. couldn't imagine a swarm of nine-and-ten-year-olds on a crowded Saturday, but Maddie didn't look even slightly fazed. "I could grill the hot dogs," he offered. They had a garden space in the back of the building. It wasn't large, but there was plenty of room for the grill, a picnic table, chairs and a swing. "What else do you want me to do?"

Maddie pursed her lips. "I'll make a list...not just for you. A list of everything we'll need to get done—decorations, favors, place settings..."

"Presents," Lillian added to their list.

Lowering her glass of milk, Chrissy smiled.

J.C. wiggled his eyebrows at her. "No peeking."

"Uncle James," she moaned. "I'm not a little kid anymore."

Oh, but she was. "Remind me…you're going to be thirty? Forty?"

Chrissy rolled her eyes.

Maddie chuckled and ruffled Chrissy's hair.

J.C. liked it when Maddie relaxed. With the shop closed and Lillian contented, Maddie shed her cloak of worry. Once upstairs in the living area, it was as though the rest of world was locked away.

He sobered, remembering Owen's intrusion. Unfortunately, not *everyone* else was locked out of her life.

Chapter Twelve

Wanting everything to be perfect for Chrissy's birthday, Maddie decided to make an investment she had been mulling over. Costumes for children's tea parties. She had planned on them when deciding to create the children's corner, but she hadn't bought them right off, having to consider the cost. As it was, buying costumes would stretch her already-mangled budget.

Fortunately, Emma McAllister had continued to frequent the Tea Cart. Before she married Seth, Emma had operated a costume shop, Try It On. Once she was married, she had sold the shop to her former assistant, Tina.

Emma came into the Tea Cart about twice a week while her twins were in preschool, often meeting friends for tea and her favorite tiny hazelnut cakes. Maddie was watching for her, wanting to discuss her idea while Chrissy was in school and couldn't overhear.

Just after ten o'clock, Emma pushed open the door, then inhaled deeply. "Fresh brewed tea and something with cinnamon. Yum."

"Apple tartlets," Maddie explained. "I just took them out of the oven. It's a new recipe I've made up, so I'm not sure how they'll turn out."

"Can I be your guinea pig?"

"Only if you let me treat."

Emma tsked. "Having been in business for myself, I can tell you that's not very profitable."

"I'm hoping to intrude on your morning quiet time, and actually it is about business."

"How can I argue?" Emma grinned. "From the aroma, those apple things have to be delicious."

Knowing Emma's favorite blend of tea, Maddie filled a teapot with leaves and boiling water. With Lillian happily chatting to one of the ladies in her Sunday school class, Maddie put the pot and cups on a small table nearby. "Is this okay?"

"Perfect."

Back behind the counter, Maddie pulled out the tray of fresh apple tartlets and stacked some on a delicate pink glass dish. She added dessert plates, forks and napkins. Unloading it all on the café table, Maddie stashed the tray.

"Is it okay for me to dive in while you talk?" Emma asked, eyeing the pastries.

"Of course."

Emma took a bite, savoring it slowly, then sighing. "Oh, I wish you hadn't come up with this recipe."

"Too sweet? Needs a touch of salt?"

"Afraid not. Now I have one more goody that'll glide from my lips to my hips."

Pleased, Maddie grinned. "Really?"

"Taste one if you dare." She took a second bite.

"If you don't mind, I'll talk instead." Maddie waved toward the nook filled with small tables. "When I was designing the shop, with Seth's inspiration, we planned an area for kids. As the idea grew, I knew I wanted to host children's parties."

"It would be great for birthday parties," Emma mused. "Girls especially."

"My thought, too. When I asked Chrissy who she wanted to invite, I thought it would probably be all girls, but she wants to invite her whole class. That got me thinking. I'd been envisioning fancy costumes for the girls, hats, gloves, fun things they don't usually have. And when Chrissy mentioned the boys, I thought, why not? For costumes, I wondered about top hats."

"And little vests," Emma mused. "Boys like lots of pockets so we could design them with extra ones. The bow tie could be sewn to one side and attached with velcro on the other."

"It's doable?"

"Sure. Great thing about costumes, you're really only limited by your imagination. We never designed any outfits with special effects like fireworks, but just about everything else, including a dragon whose eyes light up. One of the main customers for Try It On is the local theater." The theater costumes, along with Emma's award-winning designer wedding gowns, had put her shop on the national map.

Maddie quietly clapped her hands together. "Perfect! I want Chrissy's birthday to be really, really special."

"I keep her in my prayers," Emma said quietly. "Such an enormous loss for a little girl."

"Fortunately she has her uncle."

"And you."

Maddie shook her head. "I don't do much."

Emma stared at her. "You're kidding. Chrissy has improved by leaps and bounds since you've been in her life."

"She's still traumatized."

"Healing takes a long time. I know that from personal experience." Emma had come to Rosewood after being placed in the witness protection program. Formerly a prosecuting attorney, she had been targeted by the brother of someone she had rightfully sent to prison. Out for revenge, the man had tried to kill her by setting her house ablaze. She hadn't been in the house, but tragically her husband and young daughter were. Fortunately, the arsonist was caught in Rosewood when he made a second attempt on Emma's life. Pain had been tempered by her faith, but the loss was still part of who she was. Not turning it into anger, instead she had funneled it into compassion.

Knowing Emma's past, Maddie regretted stirring up any memories. "I didn't mean to—"

Emma patted her hand. "With solid people like you and J.C., Chrissy's on the right road. I can see the Lord's hand in bringing you together."

"I pray you're right." Maddie knew her own contribution hadn't been much, but she was overjoyed that Emma saw a visible difference in Chrissy. "And you can understand why the party is so important, why I want her life to be as normal as possible."

"Of course." Emma set her cup back in the saucer. "What aren't you telling me?"

Maddie traced the outline of the sugar bowl with her fingers. "I had planned to add costumes either a few at a time or later on...."

"Would an installment plan help?"

Leaning forward, Maddie's anxiety spilled out. "I know it's a huge thing to ask. I can make a deposit. I just didn't know if payments would be something a costume shop offered."

Emma lifted her shoulders. "In special circumstances. That's how I sold the business to Tina. She makes payments. I'll speak to her and we'll work out something."

Maddie suddenly realized she didn't even have a bid on how much everything would cost. It could be far more than her budget would handle.

But Emma anticipated the request. "I'll make some sketches, get Tina's input and ask her to put together a bid." She pursed her lips. "I have some vintage hats, too. Some are at the shop, some at home. The top hats will be easy to make. They don't have to be wedding-quality, especially because the boys will no doubt be pulling them off and jamming them back on. A crushable thick felt fabric might be just the thing."

"I can sew," Maddie inserted, thinking she might be able to hold down the cost.

"In all your copious spare time?" Emma shook her head. "That's about as practical as having high tea in the costume shop. Buttons in the pastries wouldn't be that appetizing."

Chuckling, Maddie was awfully glad she knew Emma. "You're right. Oh, and in the bid…I want Chrissy's dress and hat to be extra special."

"Favorite color?"

"Purple. We painted her room lavender and she really likes it."

"Hmm. Accented with red it's festive, with gold it's glamorous or royal, like a princess. For a ten-year-old girl…" Clearly, Emma's wheels were spinning.

Maddie suddenly remembered Emma's children. "I don't expect you to take time away from your kids to work on this."

"I design costumes for their school plays, anything I get a chance to. The shop's truly Tina's now, so when I can get my hands on a pencil to sketch, watch out!"

Maddie's grateful smile crinkled her entire face. "Wonderful!"

"I'll talk to Tina after I leave here." She reached for another apple tartlet. "But I'm not going until we finish our *experiment* down to the last crumb."

Maddie thought Tina's bid was very reasonable so she paid fifteen percent down on the order. Emma insisted on designing Chrissy's dress and she consulted with Maddie on the details. The end result was a swirl of multilayered lavender chiffon. The puffy sleeves were accented with cutouts edged in dainty lines of gold. She used the same effect on the high collar. It was at once age-appropriate, yet magical.

They assembled different gift bags for the girls and boys. Afterward, Maddie took Chrissy to Barton's shoe store. The owner had special ordered gold Mary Janes to go with Chrissy's party dress. Maddie wouldn't reveal the final dress design, but told Chrissy the shoes would be perfect for her outfit. Intrigued by the shiny shoes and new white tights, Chrissy was appeased.

With Tina's encouragement, they decided that choosing and putting on the costumes would be the first portion of the party. And to make this first, most important party extra special, they would gather at the Tea Cart, then walk down Main Street to the costume shop and change into their outfits. That way, if there were any fitting difficulties, Tina would have all her supplies at hand. Both Maddie and Tina thought the kids would be intrigued by a tour of the costume shop with all its nooks and crannies filled with everything from Little Red Riding Hood to dinosaurs.

Even though Chrissy was trying to play it cool, she was excited about her party. Maddie was pleased with almost everything. Except J.C.

He politely listened to her suggestions. But he didn't share anything or encourage any discussion. She knew it wasn't just her imagination. J.C. had become distant and she didn't know why.

Saturday afternoon, the children swarmed the costume shop, all clamoring to get into their party outfits. The boys were enthralled with the dinosaur costumes Tina had shown them, but the girls were more interested in princess and fairy gowns. Controlled chaos was the best way to describe their time at Try It On.

Chrissy had gotten ready at home, delighted when Maddie and Lillian presented the frothy lavender chiffon dress. The final touch was the hat Emma made. She had pleated the same lavender chiffon on the base, then added deep purple ribbon and delicate gold edging. For whimsy, she attached two jaunty feathers which she had dyed deep purple. Chrissy positively glowed when she looked in the mirror at the complete effect. As the guests arrived, the girls oohed and aahed seeing the magical dress.

For the first time, Chrissy had left the building without her backpack. She didn't even seem to notice she had. It took a while, but once all the kids had their costumes and accessories, they headed back to the Tea Cart. Crossing her fingers, Maddie hoped J.C. would be pleased. And maybe, just maybe, he would let down at least part of the barrier he had put between them.

J.C. practically flew to the Tea Cart. He had been called to the hospital in the middle of the night for an emergency that had him operating for hours. His patient now stabilized, J.C. was finally able to get back home for the party.

He dashed upstairs for a fast shower, then changed into a fresh shirt and jeans. Taking time only to shave and run a comb through his hair, he was back downstairs in ten minutes. One thing about being a doctor, his internship and then residency had prepared him to get ready in record time.

Exhaling, he saw that the kids hadn't returned yet from getting their costumes. Samantha manned the counter and Lillian sat in her special spot. The children's nook was decorated with tiny white fairy lights along with banners and balloons in Chrissy's favorite colors. A bouquet of lavender, purple and acrylic gold balloons were tied to the chair he guessed would be the birthday girl's. He hadn't pictured anything so festive.

"Looks great, doesn't it?" Samantha asked. The shop was quiet with customers at only three tables.

"Amazing."

"Wait until you see what else Maddie has whipped up."

"What can I do?"

"Light the grill," she replied. "When the kids get here, we'll be too busy to even think."

He thought she was exaggerating. "Little girls aren't all that rowdy. Boys probably won't even show up."

"Oh, you are a dreamer, J.C."

"You think they will?"

"They met here at the shop, remember? They all came."

Frowning, J.C. glanced over at the children's area. "Then we need more space for the party."

She waved her hand in dismissal. "Nope. Maddie thought out every detail. She had an exact count, then planned for a few extras. She's been planning, decorating, cooking and baking ever since Chrissy decided where she wanted her party. She wants it to be extra special."

Because this was Chrissy's first birthday without her parents. "I'll get the grill going, then round up the ketchup and mustard."

"Just the grill. Maddie already fixed a condiment bar for the hot dogs."

He frowned.

"What's wrong?"

"I'm wondering when she had time to sleep," he muttered. "Running the shop, taking care of Lillian and Chrissy..."

"She wants to do this," Samantha replied in a quiet voice. "Surely you know by now that Maddie's happiest when she's giving and caring for others. It's rare...she's rare, and special."

He knew that. Unfortunately, he wasn't the only man with that information.

The bell jangled over the door as two women entered.

"I'd better get back to work," Samantha told him, turning to greet the customers.

It didn't take long for J.C. to light the grill. A cooler sat on top of the picnic table. He flipped it open—the hot dogs. Maddie hadn't left anything to chance. He went back inside just in time to see the shop door fly open. Kids crowded inside, all dressed up. Looking closer, he saw they all looked like little ladies and gentlemen, outfitted for a formal event. Grinning, he wondered how the boys liked that. Then Chrissy stepped forward. J.C.'s breath caught.

His little Pinker Belle looked so pretty. Dressed in what he guessed was any young girl's fantasy dress, there wasn't a trace of sadness in her face.

"Uncle James!" She twirled around. "Do you like it?"

"It's very pretty..." He felt a lump in his throat. "*You're* very pretty."

Chrissy glanced down, looking shy, then tapped her shoes. "I never had gold shoes before."

Or a small but perfect hat. It was obvious everything she wore had been carefully designed. "Perfect for the birthday girl."

She grinned. "Maddie fixed everything. Isn't it cool?"

"Yep." He remembered his feeble effort of simply lighting the grill and suppressed a grimace. Good thing Maddie had picked up the ball, then scored touchdown after touchdown.

As though his thoughts had produced her, he spotted Maddie in the crowd, shepherding the kids inside. He stepped to one side so they could pass. She looked a little flushed but completely in control. Not harried or overwhelmed as he would have been. Glancing up, she met his gaze, then prodded the boy in front of her toward the small tables. J.C. would have liked to read what was in her eyes, but her gaze had darted away too quickly.

"Come on, Chance, there's plenty of room." Keeping her attention on the children, Maddie didn't look at J.C. again.

He wanted to tell her how terrific everything looked, how great she'd been organizing all of this, how grateful he was that she had put a bright smile on Chrissy's face. Instead, he watched as she herded the children to the tables.

"You probably want to get the hot dogs going," Samantha reminded him, nodding toward the back.

"Right." It didn't take long to grill the handmade hot dogs that Maddie had purchased from the local sausage maker. He found bratwurst at the bottom of the cooler, his favorite.

The kids had begun on the homemade pizzas when he brought up the plump, fresh hot dogs. As predicted, the boys dove in. The girls remained fascinated by the tiny sandwiches in the shapes of hearts, diamonds and shamrocks.

J.C. glanced at the condiment bar. As he did, the sketch on the wall above the dispensers caught his attention. Peering closer, he realized the subject was Maddie when she was probably around Chrissy's age. She was sitting at a child-size table. Dolls and a teddy bear sat in the other chairs. Miniature dishes were set on the table. *A tea party?* It must be. The young Maddie was holding a cup midair. Apparently, little tea parties had been part of her childhood. And her father had captured the scene brilliantly.

"Excuse me," Maddie said in a quiet voice.

J.C. realized he was blocking the aisle and moved aside. Before she could escape, he caught her elbow. "Tell me what to do."

Her eyes flickered in astonishment.

"I want to help with the party," he explained.

The emotion in her eyes flitted away. "Um, collect dirty dishes, um, yes, that would help."

Now she seemed plenty distracted. Before he

could voice the thought...or anything else, Maddie scurried away, disappearing in the back.

He bused the table, listening to the children's chatter. It was easy to see they were having fun. No doubt the novel type of party would catch on.

Carrying the dishes he'd collected into the kitchen, J.C. paused when he saw the birthday cake. It was a beauty. Lavender and purple around the woven sides, with pink lettering and gold candles. "Wow."

Maddie turned from the sink where she was washing her hands. "So it looks okay?"

"It looks fantastic. How did you get it all smooth on top like that?"

"Fondant over the butter cream frosting," she explained.

"Looks like it came from a fancy bakery."

"Fingers crossed, it tastes good."

J.C. scrunched his forehead in surprise. "You've never made anything that didn't taste good."

Maddie blushed. "I hope the public agrees with you."

"Have you had any complaints?"

She shook her head.

"I think I made a good investment."

Her eyes, now a soft blue, widened. "Investment?"

"As a silent partner."

She blinked, then turned back to the sink. "Good."

Frowning, J.C. wondered what he'd said wrong. "You can take that stack of dessert plates out to the party if you'd like," she continued, still not turning around.

"Sure." Each little plate was topped with a scalloped paper doily, like the ones she used for her pastries. She had seen to every minuscule detail.

"There's a tray on the counter with forks. You can stack the plates on it and save a trip."

And get out of her way? J.C. followed her instructions, leaving the kitchen. He set the tray on the counter while he collected more dirty dishes from the party nook. He couldn't very well leave the mess in the shop, J.C. rationalized as he returned to the kitchen. Maddie was checking the candles and it occurred to him that the tiered cake was probably heavy.

After depositing the dishes in the sink, he crossed the room to stand beside her. "I'll carry the cake."

"I'm used to—"

"It's too heavy for you." Surprising her, he lifted it off the counter. Before she could recover, he headed out front, pausing at the counter. "Where do you plan to light the candles?"

"Here is good." She rummaged in a drawer and produced a fireplace lighter, one long enough to reach all the candles without getting singed. Once they were all lit, J.C. headed to the table, Maddie and Sam trailing just behind him.

"Maddie! It's so pretty!" Chrissy exclaimed.

The kids and handful of adults erupted in applause. Maddie's face flushed, then she smiled. The women beamed. They all began singing "Happy Birthday," prodding Chrissy's shy grin.

"Make a wish!" Lillian called out.

Chrissy looked up.

J.C. nodded, then winked.

Maddie smiled. "Yes, make a wish!"

Chrissy closed her eyes for several moments, took a deep breath and blew out her candles.

"Yea!" Clapping her hands, Maddie left J.C.'s side to help serve the cake.

Once all the kids had some cake, she slipped an arm around Chrissy, giving her an affectionate hug before tugging her ponytail.

The curling in his stomach had nothing to do with all the delicious aromas in the shop. It had everything to do with Maddie. The way her eyes crinkled when she grinned, the laughter that was as natural to her as breathing. She had brought joy into their lives when he had thought it was impossible. Was it possible there was even more ahead? Even more to fill his heart?

Chapter Thirteen

The backyard didn't have much of a garden. But in the late spring, scents of neighboring gardens stirred in the mild breeze. The building blocked almost all of the noise from Main Street. In the evening, most people were home, reducing even that small bit of noise. Closing her eyes, Maddie could imagine that she was back at the house she had grown up in, nestled in its serenity. Amazing how much had changed in such a relatively short time. When the year began, she couldn't have imagined she would be running the Tea Cart, living in the Wagner Hill building. She certainly couldn't have imagined the way J.C. had tumbled her feelings, totally uprooted her emotions.

She pushed the wooden swing with her foot, allowing the slow motion to ease her mind. It had been some day. Chrissy's party had been all she had hoped for and more. Seeing her truly smile was such a blessing. Remembering the curt, fractious child she had first met, Maddie pondered the change. She couldn't take the credit. Actually her mother had been the one to breach the child's defenses.

Leaning her head back, Maddie studied the blanket of stars above. She had heard people scoff about the legend of the Texas skies. Although her travels had been limited, she had always studied the night skies, seeing how different the heavens looked. Maybe she was just a Rosewood girl to the bone. The thought made her chuckle.

"What's so funny?"

Startled, she sat up straight, stopping the swing's motion. "J.C., you nearly made me jump out of my skin."

"I seem to have that effect on you."

More than he knew. Certainly more than the rush of fear from running into him in an empty apartment. Far more.

"Can I sit down?"

Scooting farther over to one side, Maddie nodded.

"It's quiet out here at night," J.C. commented as he sat down.

Maddie tried not to think of his proximity, the length of his leg pressed next to her, the muscled arm that met hers.

He didn't say anything for minutes, the creaking of the swing the only discernable sound in the secluded garden. Maddie swiped nervous hands against her skirt as she tried to think of something neutral to say, something that wouldn't make him aloof.

"Quite a party today," J.C. told her.

"I think Chrissy liked it."

"Understatement." He looked up at the sky. "Only gravity kept her attached to the planet. She was floating on happiness all day."

Maddie was silenced by the poetry of his words... the appreciation.

"I didn't realize until today how much work a party is. I don't know how you made the time."

She shrugged. "I'm used to fitting a lot of different things into a day."

"Again, an understatement." He shifted, brushing her arm with his.

She swallowed.

"I almost forgot we have this little garden." J.C. glanced at the border of fuchsia and white azaleas. "I used to wonder why my mother poured so much time and energy into flowers that only bloomed two or three weeks a year. I know some varieties bloom for months, but ours didn't. Looking at them now..."

Maddie's gaze followed his. Between the light on the roof and the shimmer from the moon, she could see the delicate flowers. "The blossoms don't have to live forever. Every time I look at the bushes, I can picture the blooms long after they've fallen off."

"That doesn't surprise me."

She wondered what he meant. "I'm not sure—"

"You always try to see the best in every person and every thing."

Maddie inhaled deeply. "You think so?"

"You don't?"

Her throat dried.

"Maybe it's a Pollyanna complex..." he continued.

Jerking her chin up, she stared at him, wondering if he was teasing or mocking her.

"And maybe you're just a good person."

"I think I like the last description best." She'd intended to make the words crisp, instead her voice sounded husky.

J.C. leaned a fraction closer. "Me, too."

Was it the moonlight? Or the whisper of the stars? It couldn't be her attraction to J.C., the way he made her heart yearn, or her breath to shorten. Swallowing, she closed her eyes tight against the feelings that swamped her.

Yet she still sensed his hand hovering over hers. Along with the exquisite torture of wondering whether he would take it in his. When his fingers curled over hers, she gradually opened her eyes and slowly turned to meet his. Was that promise she saw in them? Afraid to look, even more afraid to turn away, she wondered. And hoped.

And prayed her hope wasn't in vain.

The days flew by. Chrissy, buoyed by a new attitude, continued her nature outings with J.C. and

Maddie. Heartened by the success, Maddie suggested attending Girl Scouts again. Together they looked over the list of junior badges and decided to try Camp Together first. Samantha offered her large backyard and Emma brought over a tent.

Chrissy decided to invite Lillian, Samantha, Emma and her best friend, Lexi. Although Lillian couldn't stay in the tent through the night, Chrissy wanted her to have dinner and roasted marshmallows with them. Samantha had prepared her guest room so Lillian could have a comfortable night. Emma planned to stay for part of the evening and then go home to be with her children.

That left Maddie in charge of the girls. She thought of the campouts in her own backyard as a child. Her parents always made them special, memorable. By the time darkness fell, she imagined they were in a faraway, exotic spot. In the morning she was always surprised to find she was still in her own yard. She wanted to make the same kind of memories for Chrissy.

Knowing Chrissy loved beanie weenies—pork 'n' beans with sliced hot dogs—Maddie prepared them ahead, needing only to warm the pot on Sam's grill.

The campout was on Friday night. J.C. had to follow up on two surgical patients from that day, so Bret and Seth did the heavy lifting. They carried the fire pit from the patio so the girls could use it like a campfire, and then they set up the tent. Maddie thought the four-person tent was the perfect size—they could all fit inside, but it was small enough to be cozy.

The fire flickered cheerfully as they began dinner.

Sam took a bite, then lifted her eyebrows. "Beanie weenies, huh? I didn't know what to expect, but these are good."

Emma agreed. "Tastes like baked beans...I've made this and it never turns out...so good."

"Maddie makes it special," Chrissy informed her. "With stuff besides the beans and hot dogs."

Emma shook her head, ruminating. "Obviously it's the *stuff* that makes the difference."

"I just fiddle with the ingredients," Maddie replied.

"Next time you're fiddling, write down the recipe. My kids will be grateful," Emma said, then took another bite.

Smiling, Samantha caught Maddie's gaze, then subtly nodded toward Chrissy.

Maddie could guess what her friend was thinking. Chrissy looked happy, unconcerned, like any other ten-year-old. *Thank you, Lord.* He was bringing Chrissy around, healing her pain, giving her hope. Swallowing, Maddie realized how much the child had come to mean to her. She couldn't imagine how empty her life would be without Chrissy. Her stomach wrenched as she thought of the day J.C. would meet the right woman, get married, no doubt move away.

Samantha leaned close to whisper. "Are you okay?"

"Of course. Just glad we're all together."

Her friend didn't look completely convinced, but she couldn't delve deeper with the circle of women and girls listening.

As the sun set and darkness cloaked their little gathering, they chose sticks from the pile of mesquite that Samantha had collected. The girls were first to push their marshmallows on their sticks and hold them over the fire.

Maddie brought the makings for s'mores and she helped Lexi and Chrissy assemble their treats. She turned to the other women. "S'more?"

"Yes, please," Lillian agreed instantly.

Emma groaned. "I'll have to walk ten miles to wear all this off, but yes, I want one."

Samantha shook her head. "I'm a purist, no graham crackers or chocolate." She held her long stick over the fire. "I like my marshmallows almost incinerated."

Munching on their goodies, the evening quieted around them as neighbors settled into their houses and the already-lazy streets emptied.

"Stories," the girls chanted together.

Lillian eagerly took the challenge first, telling them the story of how Rosewood had been founded by German, Czech and Polish immigrants. Her voice was dreamy as she spoke, remembering tales her parents had passed down to her.

Maddie's heart filled with joy seeing her mother

so happy. J.C.'s treatment had improved her life beyond measure. Another blessing.

Night deepened and the stories segued into the scary variety. Nothing ghoulish, just enough to cause a few goose bumps. When Sam finished her second tale, she nudged Maddie. "Your turn."

Taking a deep breath, Maddie looked at the girls' expectant faces and began.

J.C. opened the door of his apartment. The shop downstairs had been shuttered, closed for the evening campout. Shrugging out of his jacket, he tossed it on the leather club chair. One Maddie had picked out, he mused, surprised the thought had sprung up. It had been a long day of surgery, office calls and hospital rounds. And he hadn't had time to do more than grab half a sandwich. Wandering into the kitchen, he opened the refrigerator. A sticky note with his name was secured to a foil-covered plate. Funny, he hadn't really eaten that often in his own apartment. Maddie cooked all their meals. Breakfast before school and work, dinner when they converged after their separate days.

Accustomed to a welcoming smile and a warm dinner, it was surprisingly quiet in the apartment. He peeled back the foil and stuck the plate in the microwave. When the timer beeped, he carried his dinner into the living room. The chicken enchiladas that Maddie had cooked for him were good, but he didn't have much of an appetite any longer. Considerate of her to think of his dinner when she had the whole campout to get ready.

Picking up the remote control, he flipped between channels, not seeing anything that held his interest. He clicked off the television. Again, the silence was disconcerting. No chatter from Chrissy. No laughter or snatches of murmured conversation from across the hall. Sighing, he realized this was how it would be someday. Chrissy would grow up, go away to college. Maddie…he didn't want to even consider where she might be then. An image of her with Owen Radley flashed in his mind. The man wasn't good enough for her. Not that he wanted to think of her with any other man, either.

Getting up from the club chair, J.C. paced the living room, pausing at the fireplace, remembering how they had discovered the first one in her apartment, crashing through the crumbling Sheetrock. How soft she had felt in his arms. And how soft her hand had been curled in his the night of Chrissy's party.

J.C. knew the thoughts would just torture him. Glancing over at the study alcove she had fixed up for him, he considered passing the evening catching up on paperwork. The thought held no appeal.

The emptiness of his home was as blaring as a siren. He'd lived on his own for years before Chrissy had become his responsibility. And he'd never had any trouble relaxing or finding plenty to do when he was alone. Two books sat on the coffee table, ones he had been meaning to read when he had some spare time. He picked up the text on parenting. Although he had been keen to study it, the pages didn't hold his interest. Maybe something lighter, the novel he had wanted to savor on a lazy evening. Switching books, he concentrated on the words. After ten minutes, he had reached only the bottom of the first page and he didn't have a clue what he had read. *What was wrong with him?*

Getting up, he forgot about the book in his lap and it thudded to the floor, the sound overpowering in the silence. An image of Maddie's smile flashed in his thoughts. When she was planning this evening's campout, she'd been so excited that a person might have thought *she* was the junior Girl Scout. And she had been disappointed to learn he had to be at the hospital and couldn't attend the first part of the evening.

J.C. glanced across the hall. The door to Maddie's apartment was closed. Normally it was only closed at bedtime. Chrissy ran between both places as though it was one home. He supposed it was…when Maddie was there to make it so.

Maddie drew out her words, building the suspense. Chrissy and Lexi leaned forward, their eyes growing bigger, the light of the fire flickering over their faces. It was just the three of them. Samantha was inside and Emma had gone home. "The old lady had one favorite thing—a quilt she had made as a young woman. She worked for a seamstress who allowed her to keep scraps of the finest materials like silk and satin. The old lady had collected them until she had enough to sew this fine, fine quilt. Her friends and neighbors always admired it. One neighbor in particular was always after her to sell it to him. But the old lady didn't want that neighbor to have it. She sensed he wanted it so he could show it off and she wanted her treasure to be appreciated. One day the old lady fell and hurt her back. Because she didn't have anyone to care for her, she had to move into a nursing home. She wasn't even able to return home to retrieve her things, most especially her quilt."

Maddie paused, thinking that could have been her own mother's fate. She cleared the lump in her throat. "Knowing this, the neighbor dashed in, took the prize quilt and hid it in his house. He spread the beautiful quilt over his bed, gloating at his success, finally turning off his lamp so he could sleep. His eyelids closed…." Maddie drew out the words slowly, building the girls' expectations. "Just as he was falling asleep, the quilt began to creep, ever so slowly, moving toward the end of the bed. He tugged at it, thinking the fine silk and satin was just sliding because of its slickness. He closed his eyes and the quilt crept away again. Reaching to tug at the quilt, he realized it was out of his reach. His eyelids flew open! And he sat up in bed and watched as the quilt continued creeping until it fell to the floor."

She paused for effect. "Deciding he was being silly, the man fetched a rough woolen blanket to place between his top sheet and the quilt. Settling back down he closed his eyes, determined to sleep the best he ever had, now that he possessed the quilt. Sleepy again, he started to drift off when the quilt ever so slowly began to creep down."

The girls swallowed, their eyes huge.

"He suddenly remembered the old lady's words—that the quilt knew its rightful master and it would never be him…."

Chrissy's mouth dropped open a bit.

"So…" Maddie stared at the girls "…the quilt began to crawl…."

Lexi and Chrissy huddled together.

Maddie lunged forward. "And landed right here!"

The girls jumped back as though expecting the quilt to materialize, scrambling to get away.

Laughing, Maddie hugged them both. "But we know that quilts can't crawl."

"You sure?" a deep male voice asked from close by.

Shrieking, Maddie and the girls leaped as though embers from the fire pit had scorched them.

J.C. chuckled. "Didn't mean to scare anyone."

Chrissy stomped her feet. *"Uncle James!"*

"Sorry, Pinker Belle, I just thought I'd come check on you, see how everything's going."

Maddie clutched her chest, trying to catch her breath. "I thought you had to be at the hospital."

J.C. shrugged. "Got done."

Their small faces scrunched in annoyance, the girls frowned at him.

"Didn't mean to interrupt..." He took one step backward.

Recovering, Maddie shook her head. "You aren't. We were just telling scary stories."

His face eased into a smile. "I heard."

Embarrassed, Maddie flushed, grateful for the darkness that disguised it. "Come sit down by the fire. We have plenty of marshmallows to roast."

"I didn't think I was hungry, but that sounds good."

She frowned. "Didn't you find the plate I left for you?"

"By the time I got home...I wasn't in the mood to eat."

"But you're hungry now?"

"Seems like it."

"We didn't have a fancy dinner, but we have plenty." She crossed the yard to the grill where she'd kept the pot over ebbing embers. "This is still warm." Scooping out a generous portion, she handed him a paper bowl and fork.

J.C. took a bite. "What is this?"

"Beanie weenies," she explained.

He took a second bite, then a third. "This is really good."

"It's pretty simple compared to the enchiladas."

"Maybe so, but it really hits the spot." He finished off the bowl, then asked for another serving which he finished in record time.

Across the campfire, the girls had begun to droop, although they were fighting sleep.

Maddie stuck marshmallows on two sticks and handed one to him. "Requisite dessert for campouts."

"Don't have to ask me twice."

Quiet descended, with only the sparks from the fire pit intruding. Nervous, Maddie tried to think of something to say. Truth was, she enjoyed the deepening shadows uninterrupted by words.

J.C. checked his marshmallow. "Hope this stick lasts long enough that I can practically burn my marshmallow."

"You, too," she murmured. "Samantha soaked the sticks in water so they would last longer."

"Clever."

"I have graham crackers and Hershey bars."

"Maybe on the next one. This smells too good." He turned the stick. "It's just about right."

Mesmerized by the length of his tall, muscled body, she forgot to watch her own stick.

"Whoa!" J.C. moved even closer, grabbing her

stick and pulling it out of the fire. "Hope you like them really well-done."

The light flicked over the cleft in his chin, his sturdy jaw-line. And her breath quickened.

He turned toward her. "Do you?"

"What?"

J.C. smiled. "Like your marshmallow well-done?" *Could she really see the gold flecks in his eyes? Or was it night magic?*

His gaze lowered and she realized his lips were only a hand span away from hers. Pewter beams of moonlight illuminated his face. *The flecks in his eyes were truly gold.* Forgetting to breathe, she inched closer.

"No!" Chrissy called out in her sleep.

Having forgotten the girls were still across from them, Maddie jerked back. Her throat worked and she struggled to speak, her words coming out in tiny puffs. "The story."

His eyes continued to search hers. "Story?"

"The scary story...about...the quilt. I should check on the girls." She swallowed. "Get them in the tent for the night."

J.C. remained silent, his eyes locked with hers.

Chrissy stirred, her bad dream apparently continuing.

"I have to..." she began.

He exhaled. "I know." But he didn't pull away. His fingers cupped her chin.

She wanted to lean into his embrace...his kiss.

Reality hit like a wash of frigid water. What was she doing?

Rising in one accelerated motion, she left his side, rushing to check on the girls. Her back to him, she wiped away the tears she couldn't stop, any more than she could suppress the splintering of her heart. To have him so close, to imagine what it would be like if they could form a family. Knowing it couldn't happen… Tears pooled, wetting her cheeks, ripping open her heart.

Chapter Fourteen

Maddie lingered over the calico pioneer dresses in the costume shop. She could picture Chrissy wearing a small version of the dress at the harvest festival, one that would match her own. Sighing, she pushed the thoughts out of her mind. Chrissy wasn't hers to outfit and it was dangerous to keep going down that road.

Since the night of the campout she was having to remind herself of that every single day, often every hour of those days. What if? she kept wondering. What if?

"You thinking about renting one of those?" Tina asked as she waved goodbye to the customer she had been assisting.

Maddie gave a quick, tight shake of her head. "Wrong time of year anyway."

"Oh, I don't know, women rent them all year long." Tina straightened the bonnet's ties. "So, what brings you here?"

Pulling a check from her pocket, Maddie extended it to her. "My second payment."

Tina held up her hands. "No need."

Baffled, Maddie drew her eyebrows together. "I don't understand."

"Your account's paid in full."

"That can't be." Then she thought of her silent partner. "Don't tell me J.C. paid it off!"

"Actually, I can't tell you anything."

Maddie stared at her.

Tina's face scrunched in apology. "The person who paid said I had to keep it anonymous. I really thought you'd know who it is."

"Well…narrowing it down can't be too difficult." Maddie ran through the abbreviated list. J.C., Samantha, possibly Emma. Realizing Tina still felt uncomfortable, Maddie tried to recover. "Hey, it's a good thing. I'm just surprised and overwhelmed. I love the costumes. I have two more tea parties booked for this weekend."

The worry didn't leave Tina's face. "You sure you're okay with this? I wouldn't have agreed otherwise. I thought it was a nice surprise."

"It *is* a nice surprise," Maddie insisted. She held up the check. "This can go a long way toward increasing the accessory inventory, which is something I've really wanted to do."

Not completely convinced, Tina gave her a half-hearted smile. "In the future, if you still want us to supply costumes, I'll check with you first on anything to do with your account."

Wishing she hadn't made Tina feel bad, Maddie reached out to hug her. "Of course this is where I'll always order my costumes. They are perfect and so is the way you've handled things. Now, don't think about it for another second, okay? Or I'll feel terrible."

Tina's face cleared. "In that case…"

"Come over later for some lunch," Maddie told her, walking toward the door. "I made some killer chicken salad."

"You don't have to twist my arm," Tina replied.

Once out on the sidewalk, Maddie's smile disappeared. What had J.C. been thinking? She wanted… no, needed to make the shop succeed. The start-up money was one thing, but he couldn't bail her out every time she made an investment in the business. What would happen when he was gone and she had to handle things on her own? The thought pierced her very being. Tears blinding her vision, Maddie rushed the rest of the way to her shop, hating that she had to confront J.C.

J.C. dashed up the stairs, eager to get home. Since the night of the campout, when he realized how lonely he was in the empty apartment, he had developed a new appreciation for everything Maddie did for them. And he resolved to put the past behind him. Maddie was nothing like his ex-wife. It had been unfair to compare them.

Shedding his jacket and briefcase in his own apartment, he could hear Chrissy's chirpy voice and the far quieter replies from Lillian. Inhaling the scent of what he guessed was roast chicken, his stomach rumbled.

"I'm winning!" Chrissy announced as he walked into the Carters' entry hall.

Glancing her way, J.C. saw that she and Lillian were playing checkers. "Watch out." He winked. "Mrs. Lillian's pretty cagey."

Chrissy scrunched her nose at him, then grinned.

He followed his nose to the wonderful aromas in the kitchen. "Smells delicious."

"Just roasted chicken and potatoes." Maddie didn't turn around, adding black olives to a bowl filled with lettuce and sliced tomatoes. "And this salad."

"Do you want me to set the table?"

"Chrissy already did it."

J.C. glanced toward the living room. "Did Chrissy give you a hard time about it?"

"No. She sets the table every day, it's one of her chores."

J.C. had barely been able to get his niece to attend school. He wished Maddie would turn around so he could see her face. Sharp beams of late-afternoon sunlight lit her strawberry-blond hair. Wanting to reach out and touch the soft waves, instead he wandered over to the refrigerator and grabbed a root beer. "What kind of salad dressing do you want?"

"I made a vinaigrette." She finally turned toward him. "Will you tell Chrissy and my mother that we're ready?"

Her face was so expressionless, he started to ask if anything was wrong, then he remembered that Lillian and Chrissy were close by. They were just finishing their game of checkers when he walked back into the living room. Chrissy hopped up and rushed into the kitchen while he offered his arm to Lillian.

"Thank you, young man," she said with old-fashioned gentility.

"My pleasure." When they reached the table, Chrissy was filling the water glasses.

As had become their habit, he blessed the food. Passing the salad around, Chrissy chattered about her day. Lillian picked the black olives from her salad and gave them to Chrissy because they were one of the child's favorites.

Maddie offered the carving knife and fork to him. He sliced some white and dark meat, severing a drumstick for Chrissy. She remained a live wire and Lillian smiled at the child's silliness. But Maddie was unusually quiet. Not silent, just quiet. Maybe she'd had a rough day in the shop. Orders sometimes went amiss and even in Rosewood customers could be cranky.

"Can I have chicken salad in my sandwich again tomorrow?" Chrissy asked.

"If that's what you want," Maddie replied.

"It's yummy." Chrissy turned to him. "Maddie puts dried cranberries in it and it's really good."

"And she uses roasted chicken instead of boiled," Lillian added. "That makes a big difference."

He glanced at the roast chicken they were having for dinner.

Maddie nodded. "It's easier if I coordinate the sandwich fillings to what we're eating for dinner."

"I'm so hungry I could have eaten a plate of boiled cabbage," he replied.

She smiled, but it was a small, reserved smile.

"But I'm glad it's chicken." He stabbed a bite. "How did things go in the shop today?"

Shrugging, Maddie reached for the potatoes. "Fine."

"Nothing out of the ordinary?" he persisted.

A strange look entered her eyes and her lips thinned to a line. "No."

He glanced over at his niece and Lillian. Whatever was on Maddie's mind would have to wait until later in the evening after both had been tucked in bed.

By the time they had eaten and Chrissy reluctantly surrendered the book she was reading, J.C. was anxious to find out what was the matter with Maddie. He tried to think of all the possibilities, but came up blank. He waited what he hoped was long enough for Maddie to get her mother settled in for the night. Chrissy was asleep, so he left only a few lights on, propping open his apartment door so he could hear if she woke up and needed him.

Maddie sat alone in her living room. The television was off and she wasn't reading as she often did.

"Lillian asleep?"

"Yes." She looked up at him. "Have a seat."

Choosing the closest chair to her, he hoped she wouldn't dance around the problem.

"J.C.," she began. Knitting her hands together, she pressed until the tips of her fingers whitened. "I went to Try It On today."

He waited.

"The costume shop," she explained.

"And?"

She glanced down, then pressed her fingers even tighter. "It was a very kind gesture, but you can't keep funding everything."

Baffled, he drew his eyebrows together.

"The costumes," she continued. "I know you paid the outstanding balance in full."

J.C. blinked.

"Tina told me."

"Maddie—"

"It's not that I don't appreciate the thought, but I have to know if the Tea Cart can succeed without a benefactor." She looked pained, upset. "I have to think of the future."

Of the dozens of possibilities that had run through his mind, this one hadn't even made it to the list. "Before you go on, I didn't pay off the costumes."

"But…" Her mouth remained open, then she bit down on her lower lip. "I was sure it had to be you."

"Nope."

Her eyes darkened. "Then who?"

He wanted to know, as well.

"I'm sorry, J.C. I just assumed…" She shook her head, short rapid nods. "I can't imagine…" She exhaled. "I feel terrible. I've been worried…well, anyway, sorry."

"You really don't have anyone else in mind?" The happiness he'd been feeling the past few weeks drained at an incredible rate.

Slowly she shook her head.

Immediately, J.C. thought of Owen Radley. The man had the money…and definitely the motive. Seeing the remorse in Maddie's eyes, J.C. wanted to discard the thought, wished it away, but it stayed, planted so firmly he knew it was all he would think about. Not even the gray in Maddie's eyes softening to blue could chase it away.

Unable to leave the Tea Cart, Maddie called Samantha who agreed to come over. Two tables of women had come in just after the shop opened and were lingering over their tea and scones. Normally, Maddie would have been delighted with the early business, but she had hoped to have the place to herself so she and Samantha could talk.

Lillian sat at her usual spot, crocheting. Every single day at least one of the ladies in her Sunday school class came by to visit.

The bell over the door jangled and Maddie was relieved to see Samantha. Dispensing with the usual niceties, she waved Samantha over.

Sam sniffed the air. "Is that the cheesecake kind of filling you put in some of the pastries?"

Maddie pulled her behind the counter.

"I was just asking," Samantha muttered. "Don't I even get tea?"

Grabbing the hot water, Maddie dumped in some of the blend she'd prepared for the last customer. "It has to steep, okay?"

"Silly me. I thought that's what we did here— drink tea and—"

"Sorry," Maddie apologized. "Of course you can have some tea. It's just…"

The teasing left Samantha's eyes. "What's wrong?"

"Nothing's wrong. But I do need to ask you something."

"Shoot."

"Sam, did you pay off my account at the costume shop?"

"What gave you that idea?"

Maddie tried to temper her impatience. "I really need to know."

"No, I didn't pay anything at the costume shop."

"You're sure?" Maddie persisted. Samantha wasn't just her best friend, she was also one of the few people who knew about her payment arrangement at Try It On.

"I think I would remember something like that!" She scrunched her brow. "Oh, I bet it was J.C."

Maddie shook her head. "I already asked him. His expression matched yours—clueless."

"Did you just insult me?"

"Funny." Maddie sighed. "Sam, *somebody* paid my account in full."

Samantha started to speak.

But Maddie cut her off. "No, Tina won't tell me. Whoever it was said they wanted to remain anonymous."

Samantha scratched her head. "And you're absolutely positive it wasn't J.C.?"

"He wants to know who did."

A knowing look settled across Samantha's face. "I bet he does."

Samantha and her happy endings. "It's not like that."

"Uh-huh." Then her expression changed to a frown. "Do you suppose it was Owen?"

"Owen?"

"Think about it. He has the money. It wouldn't

even put a dent in his wallet. And the weird way he's been acting ever since you opened the shop…"

"That's too weird even for him. Besides, how would he know about my account at the costume shop?"

Samantha's expression remained somber. "I've always heard that rich people have their fingers in every pie. At the least, they know everything that's going on. Your birthday tea parties are being talked about all over town. If I remember right, the last time he came in before Chrissy's party, you didn't have the costumes. And we know he showed up that day and must have seen them. It doesn't take a genius to make the next leap in logic. Try It On is the only costume shop for hundreds of miles."

"It's ridiculous. I told him in no uncertain terms that our relationship is completely in the past. What would he gain from this?"

"A way to worm into your life." Samantha still looked worried. "I didn't want to say anything, but I've been asking around about Owen. Since I was gone from Rosewood for years, I didn't have any idea what he'd been up to. Apparently, he's spent just about as much time away from here as I did. And I got the same answer from everybody I asked about whether he had married, gotten engaged. There hasn't been anyone in his life since you two broke up."

Maddie frowned. "He must have kept it quiet.

And maybe the woman lives somewhere else, somewhere he travels to."

"That's not the impression I got."

Noticing that one of the customers was trying to catch her attention, Maddie had to leave the speculation unfinished. Several new customers came in, so Samantha pitched in and helped. Still, it took a while to prepare the new orders. As Maddie was arranging heart-shaped sandwiches on the last plate, Emma stopped in.

Samantha noticed, too, and guided Emma to a table situated away from the other customers.

Maddie hurried, delivering the plate of sandwiches and refilling a few cups. Not wanting to look as though she was pouncing on Emma, she slowed her rapid steps. "Hi. Do you want to start with tea?"

"No. Samantha said you needed to talk. What's up?"

Maddie cringed. "Sam didn't need to say anything."

Emma looked concerned.

"Guess I'll just spit it out." Maddie took a deep breath. "Emma, did you pay off my account for the costumes? Or make some kind of arrangement with Tina so I didn't owe anymore?"

"You mean someone paid it off?"

Maddie's heart sank. "Then it wasn't you?"

"You know what? I bet J.C.—"

"He was the first person I asked. It's really got me baffled."

"Tina must know—"

"Sworn to silence. I already made her feel bad about not being able to tell me." Maddie held up her hands, ticking off each name on progressive fingers. "It's not J.C. or Samantha or you."

Sam jumped in with her suggestion. "I told her I thought it was Owen Radley."

Emma frowned. "I've heard a lot about him." Not being a native of Rosewood she didn't automatically know everyone. But there was something in her tone…

"Like what?" Maddie asked.

Emma fiddled with the salt cellar. "Seth did some business with him. Even though the Radleys have a lot of money to spend, Seth doesn't want to work for him again."

"Owen's been acting weird ever since Maddie opened the shop," Samantha confided.

Maddie sent her friend a pointed gaze.

"Well, he *has!*" Samantha insisted. "They went together in high school and college, even got engaged. When Maddie wouldn't put Lillian in a nursing home, he gave her an ultimatum—her mother or him. Now he acts as though he still has a claim on Maddie."

Worry stirred in Emma's eyes. "People like that can be dangerous. You both know what I lost…" The memory of her murdered husband and child chilled the air. "And that the guy who was after me nearly killed me here in Rosewood. I don't want to scare you, Maddie, but you never know what drives some people."

Maddie hated that she had caused Emma to think about that terrible time in her life. Good grief, she was talking about someone paying a bill, not committing murder. Clearly, she had overreacted. "Emma, I used to know Owen really well. I don't believe he would hurt me or anyone else. If anything, he's just a lot of hot air."

The worry didn't leave Emma's face. "I hope you're right." Briefly she closed her eyes, then swallowed. "And I didn't mean to scare you unnecessarily. But please be careful. I wish I could have been warned."

Maddie took Emma's hand. "I'll be careful. I promise." She made herself smile brightly. "Maybe I have a secret admirer or benefactor. I should be grateful instead of making a fuss. Now, I'm going to get tea for all of us. I've got some of those apple tartlets you like, Emma. Be right back."

Maddie brought the tea and pastries, checked on her customers and kept her smile in place. All the while she wondered. The pit in her stomach told her this wasn't over. What worried her was that her intuition was usually right on. And now it was saying trouble.

Chapter Fifteen

J.C. reworked his schedule so he could take the day off. Chrissy had a school project—to collect aquatic bugs. It was a good opportunity to connect with nature and strengthen her faith. When Chrissy invited Maddie, Samantha offered to take care of the Tea Cart so that she could join them.

Although they'd had a fair-size rainstorm earlier in the week, the sun was bright, the day clear. With underground springs from aquifers populating the land, it was easy to find creeks and streams for Chrissy's school project.

His SUV handled the hilly terrain, still they bumped along. But he didn't mind when Maddie occasionally pitched near him.

"There it is!" Chrissy sang out from the backseat.

J.C. parked and Chrissy practically flew out of the vehicle. He opened the back cargo door and started unloading everything they had packed, which was quite an assortment.

Chrissy held up her list importantly, checking the first item. "Everybody wore safe shoes." She glanced at them.

Maddie stuck out one foot clad in an old running shoe.

Chrissy looked pointedly at J.C., so he extended his waterproof hunting boot.

She checked the box on her project list. "Forceps?"

J.C. held up three pairs of tweezers.

"I have the magnifying glasses and nets," Maddie offered.

Carefully Chrissy marked those boxes on the paper. "I have the pans to hold the bugs and pencils so we can write down what we find."

"And the list," J.C. couldn't resist adding.

"And the list," Chrissy repeated seriously.

Maddie's gaze slid toward him, her lips clamped shut so she wouldn't laugh.

"Everybody needs to have forceps, a net and a magnifying glass."

Following Chrissy's directions they all swapped until everyone had one of each. Allowing Chrissy to take the lead, they followed her to the stream.

"We have to be careful," Chrissy instructed. "And when you turn over rocks to find bugs, you have to put the rocks back just like they were."

This time J.C. caught Maddie's gaze. Both glanced away so they wouldn't erupt in laughter and hurt Chrissy's feelings.

Wading into the shallow water, they each looked

for rocks to upturn. While Maddie concentrated on finding bugs, J.C. found himself concentrating on her. The bright sunshine made her strawberry-blond hair look golden. He liked the casual way it fell over her shoulders and glinted in the light. If they were panning for gold, he'd know just where to find it.

"Uncle James!" Chrissy's eyebrows pulled together in disapproval. "You have to look *under* the rocks."

So he did. Not wanting Maddie to realize he had been studying her, J.C. flipped over a rock. But he didn't slide the net carefully along the sandy bottom as Chrissy had instructed them on the drive to the stream. Instead, he wondered how Maddie felt about Owen Radley. Were they in a relationship? And if they were, why didn't she say something? Was it possible they were keeping their relationship quiet because of Lillian? Maybe Maddie didn't want Lillian to feel like a burden...that she was keeping the couple apart.

But *Owen Radley?* Just thinking about the man left a bad taste in his mouth. Maddie could do so much better. So much...

J.C. didn't hold himself up as some sort of perfect match, but he couldn't stomach the idea of Maddie with Owen. She deserved...she deserved the very best, someone who would not only love her, but cherish her, appreciate every wonderful quality she possessed. The epiphany hit him like a club to the head—it was just how he felt about Maddie. Despite his mistrust, despite her possible feelings for Owen, his feelings had grown.

But how did Maddie feel? If anything at all. An image of Owen's bullying face intruded. Blindly, J.C. reached for a rock, colliding with Maddie who was already holding the same stone. Their hands brushed and he wanted to hold hers close.

Maddie watched him, her eyes a magical mix of blue, green and gray, reflecting the water, the sky, the fields of wild grasses. Vulnerable, they exposed a glimpse into her thoughts. Or was he just imagining what he wanted to see? When she didn't pull away, he absorbed every nuance of her expression, the velvety texture of her skin, the dimple that dared him to kiss her cheek.

If his niece wasn't standing twenty feet from them, he would accept that invitation, learn for himself if her skin was as soft as it looked, her lips as welcoming.

Standing so close, he could see Maddie's throat working, the uncertainty in her trembling hands. *Share your secrets!*

"When we get enough bugs," Chrissy called out, "I have to collect some leaves for extra credit." She pointed toward the sloping hill. "From up there. I have a plastic bag in my pocket."

If he could give in to irresponsibility, J.C. would have suggested she go on her own. But it wasn't part of his makeup. "Okay."

"Did you…" Maddie began, then cleared her voice. "Did you get any bugs?"

J.C. looked down into his shallow, empty pan. "Not yet."

"Oh."

They both knew they weren't talking about bugs, but the difficult words remained unsaid.

"I found a snail!" Chrissy announced.

Maddie continued to hold his gaze.

"I'm going to write it on my sheet."

"Good idea," he replied, his voice raspy.

"Yes," Maddie agreed in a breathless whisper.

"Did you find anything yet?" Chrissy persisted.

Reluctantly J.C. withdrew his hand and straightened up so he could see Chrissy. "I'm still looking."

"I have to collect at least three," she replied. "And a sample of moss if we can find any."

Maddie's hand still shook as she turned over the rock they'd both touched. "Maybe there'll be one under here." But she glanced up at him rather than down at the creek bed.

J.C. didn't want to move, but made himself search for another rock. It took a while, but between them, they found four different bugs that Chrissy could catalog.

Wading out of the stream, Maddie nearly slipped, then righted herself. "I guess my running shoes weren't the best choice. Wrong kind of traction, I guess."

Climbing the slope to search for leaves was a

little trickier than it appeared. The rain had softened the soil, making it slippery. Chrissy clambered up like a monkey. J.C. had decent traction with his hunting boots, but he kept his pace slow to watch out for Maddie. On dry ground her shoes would have been fine. But they weren't meant to dig in to wet soil. Near the top, he turned and extended his hand.

Maddie accepted, her soft skin seeming to meld into his. He wasn't sure if the quivering he felt was in her hand or his heart.

"Look! A rainbow!" Chrissy pointed to the sky.

J.C. didn't turn, keeping his gaze on Maddie. "Yes, beautiful."

Her hand definitely trembled in his.

"Come here, you all," Chrissy insisted. "It might go away before you see it."

"I don't think so," J.C. replied so quietly that only Maddie could hear.

With the ever-changing attention of a ten-year-old, Chrissy had abandoned the rainbow by the time they looked toward the sky. She had begun scavenging for leaves. Because it was spring, there were new leaves on the trees and remnants of those that had fallen in autumn and winter. Chrissy seemed determined to collect each and every kind.

"She wants enough to fill a big poster board," Maddie whispered. "It's for extra credit, but she wants it to be the best one in her class."

The fact that his niece did was incredible. Before her turnaround, she had failed two subjects. Maddie's gentle care had healed Chrissy in a way that no psychologist's sessions could have.

"The rainbow really is something," she continued, looking upward. "I think this outing is perfect for Chrissy, for her to feel the connection between the Lord and what He created."

J.C. watched Chrissy twirl in the leaves, then reach toward one of the low-hanging branches. "I can't help wondering whether I should have taken Chrissy to more counseling. If I had, she might have started healing sooner. She didn't want to go and after refusing to speak during the first three appointments, I couldn't see much point in continuing."

"I think you did the right thing," Maddie assured him. "She needed a home, not a counselor. Since she's improving, I can't see reconsidering your decision."

"Back then, especially as a medical professional…"

"You're also her uncle and you'd just lost your sister. Being a doctor doesn't make you immune to your feelings."

"Most people think it does," J.C. admitted. "As though because I've lost patients before, it doesn't bother me when I lose another. It's a big deal every time."

"Your patients should be grateful you feel that way." Maddie's eyes, large and luminescent, filled with empathy. "Look at how you've cared for Mom. I was afraid to hope that she would stop worsening. I know it's not the same as before her stroke, but…" Her lips wobbled. "It's a miracle."

"What's a miracle?" Chrissy questioned.

"I didn't see you, sweetheart." Maddie swiped at her cheeks. "The miracle is how much better Mrs. Lillian is since your Uncle James has been taking care of her." She encircled Chrissy's shoulders with one arm. "And like the rainbow you just showed us, it's a sign of the Lord working in our lives."

Sobered, Chrissy stared at her uncle.

"Do you see it, Pinker Belle?" he asked quietly.

"I think so. I just wish…"

Maddie tightened her hold on Chrissy's shoulders. "Losing someone is really hard. When my dad passed away…it hurt. A lot. But the Lord kept watching out for us, brought you and your uncle into our lives."

Chrissy scrunched her forehead. "I still wish Mom and Dad were here."

"Of course you do! Want to know something? I still dream about my dad all the time, but in a good way. He's always happy, healthy."

"Does he smile?" Chrissy asked cautiously.

"Yes, he does."

"I had a dream sorta like that."

J.C. smoothed her hair. "Your parents would be happier knowing you trust the Lord again."

Chrissy blinked. "I want that."

Maddie took a shaky breath and met J.C.'s eyes. "You can tell the Lord about it in your prayers."

Considering this, Chrissy finally nodded. "Okay." She scampered toward a copse of slender trees.

"There's nothing as simple or complex as a child's thinking," J.C. remarked. "She questions the deepest meanings, yet can accept just like that."

"Life would be a lot less complicated if we could keep that reasoning with us as adults," Maddie mused.

J.C. wished that were true, as well. Then he could understand what was in Maddie's head, know whether he was chasing a fantasy.

"Are you guys going to help?" Chrissy called out.

The moment to ask was gone. He and Maddie headed toward the trees to pick out specimens for the poster. It didn't take very long to fill Chrissy's bag with leaves. She started toward the slope, getting ready to climb down.

"Chrissy, let's go back the way we came. The soil's not all that stable. At least we know what we faced climbing up." He led the way back to the spot above the stream. "I'll go first. That way if anyone takes a tumble, I can block you from falling all the way." The footing was mushy, but J.C. didn't have any trouble. Glancing back regularly, he could see Maddie and Chrissy following. About ten feet from the bottom, he heard an unexpected whoosh.

"Watch out!" Maddie hollered as she slipped.

He turned, seeing that she was sliding toward him rapidly. Planting his feet in a solid brace, he reached out to catch her. Although she was a small person, she was moving fast, far too fast for the waterlogged hillside.

J.C. caught her, but his feet didn't hold in the shifting soil. Clutching Maddie close, they slid the rest of the way, landing at the edge of the stream.

Maddie was in his arms. Finally. Unlike the day they'd crashed into each other in the fireplace, she didn't pull away. She was so close he could count the freckles peppering her nose, touch the softness of her cheeks, feel the whisper of her breath. Like a gift from the heavens, she was the woman he had waited for all his life.

Wanting to never let her go, he didn't turn around when Chrissy hollered, "Whoo-hoo!"

He was near enough to fit his lips to Maddie's, to see if she would reciprocate. Angling his head, he was knocked off balance when Chrissy flew on top of him, tangling her limbs with theirs. Arms, legs and torsos collided, then went askew as they all toppled into the water.

"Are you all right?" J.C. questioned his niece.

She giggled. "Uh-huh."

"Maddie?"

Maddie tried to sit up. "I think so." Rubbing her arm, she nodded. "Just bumped it against a rock."

Ignoring his emotions, J.C. examined her arm. "It's not broken, unless there's a minor stress fracture."

"Really, it's fine," Maddie insisted. "It'll probably bruise. No big deal."

J.C. turned to Chrissy. "Does anything hurt? Legs? Arms? Your head?"

"Nope. You and Maddie were good padding."

The laughter they'd held in all day exploded.

"What's so funny?" Chrissy demanded.

"Nothing, *Stinker* Belle," J.C. answered when he caught his breath. "Glad we could be of service."

She looked at them suspiciously.

"And I bet you collected more leaves than anyone else in your class," Maddie added.

Distracted, Chrissy's suspicion evaporated. "I got four kinds of bugs. Some of the boys were just going to dig up earthworms and try to find ants."

"Do you mean we didn't have to wade into the stream?" J.C. questioned.

Chrissy shrugged. "To find water bugs you do. I thought that'd be way cooler than worms and ants."

J.C. extended a helping hand to Maddie so they could stand. "Ants and worms, huh? Let's hope when she studies astronomy she doesn't have us try to hitch a ride on the space shuttle."

Maddie hummed as she cleaned one of the round tables in the shop. Monday afternoons were usually quiet, but she didn't mind. It was a good day to stock the shelves, check what she needed to order. Glancing out the front window, she saw Samantha and waved, always happy when her friend dropped by.

"Hello, Lillian!" Samantha said brightly. "How are you today?"

"I'm just fine, young lady." Lillian held up her crocheting. "As bright as this red yarn."

Samantha grinned. "And you, Maddie?"

"Sunflower yellow!"

"I think I've stumbled onto a rainbow."

Grabbing Samantha's favorite blend of tea, Maddie allowed herself a dreamy smile.

"Something I said?" Sam reached for two cups and saucers.

"Just thinking about how much fun we had on Chrissy's outing to collect bugs."

Samantha wrinkled her nose. "I love everything in a garden, but I never thought of you as the bug type."

Laughing, Maddie placed Sam's favorite cookies on a dish. "Now, I'd like to see the woman who admits to being the *bug type*."

"Fair point. Want to sit near the window? Or in the back nook? Unless Lillian's expecting company?"

"Doesn't matter."

"My, we are in a good mood." Samantha wiggled her eyebrows. "Anything you want to share?"

"Isn't it amazing how life can change without you expecting it to? In a good way, I mean?"

Samantha's eyes softened. "Like my reuniting with Bret… It's beyond amazing."

"Beyond…" Maddie precariously balanced her burgeoning emotions. "I don't think I've ever been this happy." And she never wanted the feeling to change.

Chapter Sixteen

J.C. was glad for the short lull in patients. The previous week had been packed. Punching up his calendar on the laptop, he glanced at the afternoon lineup. Frowning, he read Owen Radley's name as the first appointment after lunch. He pushed the intercom button. "Didi? Why is Owen Radley on today's schedule?"

There were a series of clicks as she referenced the schedule on her computer. "He made an appointment for a consultation."

"What are his symptoms?"

A few more clicks. "He didn't say. He specified a consultation, not an exam."

"Thanks, Didi." J.C. turned off his intercom. It wasn't difficult to guess what the other man had on his mind, and it wasn't neurological in nature. Glancing at his watch, he saw that Owen would be arriving in minutes. Too late to cancel the appointment. As much as he dreaded what the other man had to say, J.C. also wanted all the facts. He and Maddie had danced around them far too long already.

Didi knocked briskly on his door. "Mr. Radley's here, Dr. M."

Once Owen was inside, she discreetly closed the door.

"Have a seat." J.C. didn't waste a smile or words of phony cordiality.

Owen took the chair closest to J.C. "I'll get right to the point."

J.C. waited.

"I want to buy the Wagner Hill building." Owen opened his briefcase. "My attorney has drawn up an offer." He extended the papers.

"The Wagner Hill isn't for sale."

"Read the proffered amount."

J.C. reluctantly accepted the document, scanning it until he saw the proposed price. It was sixty percent over the appraised value. J.C. was certain of it because an appraisal had been necessary for the estate distribution. "Why the Wagner Hill?"

"How many buildings are for sale on Main Street?" Owen countered, clearly knowing there weren't any.

J.C. didn't believe for a minute that the offer was related to real estate.

"I intend to create a museum of living history, Rosewood's history."

"That doesn't sound very profitable."

Owen didn't blink. "I understand your skepticism. But along with wealth comes obligation. This generation of my family's legacy."

"Understandable, but as I said, the Wagner Hill isn't for sale."

"Would you rather see a superstore in its place?" Owen's already-hard eyes deadened. "Because that's the only other buyer that'll be interested. That or a T-shirt and mug shop that I suspect would draw in the tourists."

"The point's moot. If the building isn't sold, nothing has to replace it."

"Are you certain that's what your niece will decide once she's in charge of her own estate? Young women these days aren't always keen on keeping traditions in place."

"What Chrissy wants to do with the Wagner Hill is her choice and I'll respect it."

Owen leaned forward a fraction. "But are you respecting her estate now? That offer will ensure her financial future. Do you feel comfortable rejecting it out of hand?"

J.C. despised the man's smug expression, but he couldn't deny the truth in his words.

"Why don't I leave it with you for now? I'm sure the best interests of your niece will be your primary consideration." Owen rose. "I'll see myself out."

Even after Owen was gone, his oppressive imprint lingered. J.C. swivelled his chair toward the window, needing air, fresh, untainted air.

The price Owen dangled stuck in his mind as though carved of granite and painted in neon orange. It would do more than pay for Chrissy's education. Owen's offer would allow Chrissy to pursue whatever she might want, a business, travel, a charitable foundation.

And J.C. couldn't dispute the value of a living history museum. The town as a whole had decided long ago that they wanted Rosewood to retain its thriving local economy, encouraging entrepreneurs to keep their businesses. That didn't happen in towns that allowed superstores to invade, undercutting prices, driving small business owners to bankruptcy.

Rosewood didn't welcome a tourist economy, either. It was difficult to keep the integrity of their community when constantly pandering to tourists to keep afloat. Of course, some of their business partially came from tourists, like the bed and breakfast and eating places. But those businesses were locally owned. Many of the tourists they served were regulars who came back year after year because they appreciated the town's inherent difference. Wildflower season bloomed with visitors that they welcomed like old friends. But this... The prospect of changing Rosewood into a clone of other overtaken towns was bitter.

But it was the other factor, as welcome as the plague, that worried him most. How did Maddie play into this offer? Did she know what Owen was up to? That prospect was sickening. The lovely woman who had brought laughter and warmth into his home, his life… Could she have been part of this?

J.C. stayed late at the office, prolonging his arrival home. Although the shop was shuttered, as usual Maddie had left two lamps on, a soft welcoming glow. Locking the front door behind him, J.C. instantly thought of the night Owen had brazenly trespassed.

His feet dragged as he climbed the stairs. Chatter, laughter and cooking smells floated toward him. He had phoned to let Maddie know he wouldn't be home in time for dinner. She always kept a plate for him in the warming drawer of the oven. The night the ladies had all been gone to the campout flashed in J.C.'s thoughts. Lonely. The heart of the home had been gone and he had desperately missed it.

Swallowing, he wondered how he would ever fare on his own again. Stupid thought! He had lived by himself for years. But that was before he met Maddie.

As usual, the doors to both apartments were propped open. Loosening his tie, he chose to enter Maddie's first. She spotted him and smiled.

Then her gaze landed on his briefcase. "Did you bring a lot of work home?"

He took the easy way out, shifting the case in his hands. "Enough to keep me busy all night."

Her smile remained constant. "Understandable. I have inventory to work on myself."

J.C. couldn't stand making small talk when there was such an important issue to air. "Fair enough. Chrissy—"

"She's helping Mom with her crocheting." Maddie glanced over at them, lowering her voice. "I think everything's coming out circle shaped." She grinned. "Excellent pot holders."

Although he tried, J.C. couldn't force a smile. "Good practice."

Maddie met his gaze. "Is anything wrong?"

He looked at the concern in her eyes, wishing he could see straight through to her soul. "Should there be?"

"Why…no. Of course not." Maddie's smile faded as she tightened her hold on a dish towel.

"Is Chrissy okay over here for a while?"

Her brow furrowed. "Sure."

Unable to hold up his end of the conversation any longer, J.C. left. The prospect of wading through his thoughts was almost worse, but he couldn't fence with Maddie. She looked concerned, wounded. And despite Owen Radley and all his implications, J.C. couldn't bear to hurt her.

Maddie watched until J.C. disappeared inside his apartment. Although he didn't completely close the door, he pulled it from its propped open position so that barely a foot of it remained open. Why did he want to shut himself away? Torment was written in his eyes, his face, even his voice. What could it be? Thoughts whirling, she considered the possibilities. There literally was no family of his left that could be ill or in trouble. Friends? She would have heard through the grapevine about their mutual friends in Rosewood. Of course, he had friends from college and med school. Maybe…

It struck her. A patient. She remembered J.C.'s words about how losing one hurt just as much every time. Before she could change her mind, Maddie sped across the hall, knocking quietly on his door.

Silence. Then the scraping of shoes as he got up, the footfalls as he approached. J.C. pushed the door open wider.

Maddie placed one hand on his. "I know, J.C."

He stared at her with utter bleakness.

"I'm so sorry. I know how deeply this affects you."

"Maddie?" His voice was hoarse, gravelly.

"Losing a patient… I know how you suffer."

J.C. glanced down.

"I'll keep you in my prayers. I hope you can think instead about all the patients you've helped, like Samantha and Mom. Now, I'll let you be alone. But remember, you don't have to be…alone, I mean. I'm just across the hall." She patted his hand a final time, then turned to cross the hall. Oddly, she thought she felt his gaze on her back the entire time.

But not wanting to intrude on his emotions, she kept her face forward, hoping her words had helped.

As the days passed, J.C. couldn't shake Owen's insinuations. Or Maddie's overwhelming concern. Working until late every evening, he made sure he wasn't home until long after dinner was eaten. And each evening she left a special meal in his refrigerator. But his appetite had disappeared.

J.C.'s staff had begun to notice. He waved away their concern. But today Didi had brought him one of his favorites from the café, hoping to tempt him into eating. He had to do something.

Seth McAllister was his only friend who also knew Maddie fairly well. Fortunately, Seth had time to meet with him, so J.C. drove over to his current work site, an old Victorian home, to talk.

The oak-lined, brick-paved street was in the oldest part of Rosewood. Many of the homes were still lived in by descendants of the town's founders. Its permanence resonated with J.C. How would this neighborhood look in twenty years if a superstore took hold of the town? Would it eventually become run-down or deserted because the owners' businesses could no longer compete?

Seth's truck was parked out front. J.C. pulled in behind it. The place was quiet. Plans rolled out on a makeshift table, Seth sat on a crate of tile. He gestured to another one close by. "Pull up an uncomfortable hunk of wood."

"Where's your crew?"

"I told them to take an extra hour for lunch."

J.C. winced. "That wasn't necessary."

Seth unscrewed the lid on a thermos bottle. "I can enjoy an hour with an old friend." He poured coffee into two foam cups.

J.C. straddled the extra crate, then picked up a cup.

Seth sipped his coffee, letting J.C. begin at his own pace.

"Do you know Owen Radley?"

"Why?"

"It's important, Seth."

"I did one job for him. He undercut the price we agreed on, imposed penalties that weren't in the contract, made up restrictions so he could charge the penalties. Worse, he treated my men…poorly."

J.C. told Seth about Owen's offer to buy the building.

"Wagner Hill? Nothing personal, but what does he want with the building? I appreciate the fine craftsmanship, the history of the place, but I'd be surprised if he does." Seth pulled his eyebrows together. "There's more, isn't there?"

"A lot. He wants to turn Wagner Hill into a living history museum of Rosewood and he'll pay plenty for the privilege."

Seth frowned. "That doesn't sound like something he'd be interested in."

J.C. nodded in agreement. "But he has a valid point about Chrissy's future. His offer is sixty percent over the highest appraisal from top market years."

"Jay and Fran left enough money for college, didn't they?"

"With their life insurance."

Seth was quiet.

"So you're wondering why I'd consider the offer? Why Chrissy would need the money? I don't know that she will. But it would give her any opportunity she could dream of."

"That she won't have otherwise?" Seth shifted his weight and the crate creaked beneath him. "Don't you believe the Lord will give her endless opportunities?"

"That goes without saying."

"Not always."

"For me it does." J.C. exhaled. "There's something else. Owen says he'll make sure we don't get a superstore on Wagner Hill's land, or a tourist shop."

"Funny, I'd have thought bringing a superstore to Rosewood would be right up his alley."

J.C. nodded.

"That's not what's bothering you."

He smiled bleakly. "You always see right to the heart of things. I don't know what Owen and Maddie...if they're in a relationship."

"Not one I've heard about and Emma usually sniffs out that sort of thing pretty well. Claims it has to do with designing wedding gowns, that she's tuned into romance." Seth paused. "Have you asked Maddie?"

"Owen's made…insinuations."

"I bet he did," Seth scoffed.

J.C. stared at the ground. "Do you think she could have planned this buyout with him?"

"Have you met the woman?" Seth shook his head in disbelief. "Think about it. A diabolical plan? First step, taking her mother to you. Of course she'd have to know that you'd offer to help her set up a shop and renovate the apartments. Then, have Owen buy the place? Kind of a stupid plan. Why use all that time and energy if Owen wanted to turn Wagner Hill into a museum? I don't think much of Owen, but from experience, he doesn't throw his money away. If anything, he would try to drive the price down." Seth frowned more deeply. "I don't like the sound of any of this."

"The man's arrogant, but I don't think he's dangerous."

Seth's face was still grim. "I know firsthand that danger comes in all kinds of packages. Even to Rosewood."

"I may be gullible, but my concerns about the danger are more…emotional than physical."

"Don't take things at face value, J.C. Talk to Maddie, find out for yourself how she feels about Owen."

"I don't have any claims on her."

"An even better reason to ask. Maybe it's time you do."

J.C. looked sharply at his friend.

"Even I can see that you're crazy about her. And Emma will tell you I'm usually the last one to know."

Maybe.

But this time, J.C. reasoned, he was the last to know.

J.C. held Seth's advice close for days. If he questioned Maddie, he had to be prepared to share his own past, explain why it was so hard for him to trust. By the end of the week he decided he couldn't put it off any longer and returned home in time for dinner.

Maddie greeted him with a hopeful smile. "I'm so glad you don't have to work late. We've missed you."

Chrissy spotted him. "Uncle James!" Putting down her book, she ran to his side. "You haven't been home in *forever*."

"Not so long," he replied, giving her shoulder a quick hug.

"You missed your turn to pick out what we do on Saturday!" She grinned mischievously. "So I got to pick."

"Hopefully we're not climbing the water tower."

Chrissy giggled. "No, silly."

"Your uncle's probably tired and hungry," Maddie intervened. "Why don't you help me dish up the vegetables?"

J.C. wandered into the living room. Lillian was crocheting something in a fine ivory yarn. Her hands trembled only slightly, a sign that she was holding her own. "Evening, Mrs. Carter."

Looking up, she tsked. "Sit down, you look as tired as week-old bread."

Her words brought a reluctant smile and he sat on the end of the sofa closest to her chair.

Lillian reached into her yarn bag, rustled around, retrieved a roll of Life Savers and handed it to him.

Accepting one, he extended the rest to her.

But Lillian waved him away. "Appears you can use the whole roll."

Even though he knew every facet of her neurological history, he sometimes saw insights in Lillian that defied her medical condition. "What about you and Chrissy?"

She dove back into her yarn bag and pulled out another roll.

Chuckling, he relaxed. "As long as you're covered."

Lillian sniffed, catching the scent of what Maddie was cooking. "Dinner ought to be ready pretty soon, shouldn't it?" She frowned. "Wouldn't be lunch I don't think..."

"Dinner," he confirmed. "Smells good."

"My Maddie's a wonderful cook, always has

been. When she could barely see the top of the kitchen table, she wanted to roll out biscuits and stir cake batter. Her father built her a special little set of stairs so she could reach. He was afraid she'd fall off a step ladder."

Chrissy ran into the room. "Dinner's ready! Come on, Uncle James, Mrs. Lillian!"

J.C. got up, then offered his hand to Lillian. Accepting, she leaned on him as they walked to the table. He pulled out her chair, then helped her get settled.

He thought about the blessing while they all assembled. Bending his head, he silently prayed for guidance. "Lord, we thank You for this nourishment, the blessings You bring us every day, for each of our loved ones. Let us appreciate these blessings, and keep in mind You are with us in each step, each day. Amen."

A quiet murmur of *amen*s circled the table.

Glancing up, he met Maddie's gaze. She sat across from him, watching, her eyes simmering with questions. Tonight they were the softest of blues, their dark-rimmed edges making them more luminescent, more enchanting.

"I've read more books than everybody in class except Susan Porter. But she reads *all* the time, even during lunch." Chrissy passed him the basket of rolls. "And she didn't do the extra credit in science."

Lillian winked at her. "You'll catch up."

J.C. felt himself thawing.

"That's right," Maddie agreed. "You made the best poster in class. And your teacher's going to enter it in the science fair."

Chrissy grinned.

The phone rang.

Maddie started to rise, but Chrissy jumped up first. "I'll get it." She scampered into the kitchen and was back in a flash. "It's for you, Maddie."

"I wonder who's calling at dinnertime," she mused.

"Owen," Chrissy replied, reaching for potatoes. "Ra…Ra something."

Startled, Maddie quickly put her napkin on the table and pushed back her chair. "I won't be a minute."

She could take an hour, J.C. told himself. A day, a week, a year. Because he didn't want to hear what she had to say about Owen Radley.

"Owen," Lillian mused. "Maddie's fiancé. Nice young man."

The sinking in J.C.'s gut nearly did him in.

It was true, then. And there was nothing he could do about it.

Except prepare to say goodbye.

Chapter Seventeen

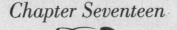

Maddie paced the cobbled walk in the far northern corner of Rosewood's town park. Away from the swings and slides, even the picnic tables, the spot was sheltered by the low-hanging branches of an ancient oak tree. The curving wrought-iron bench beneath the tree was a beacon for couples young and old, a place to sit and hold hands, to declare their love.

Owen's phone call the previous night kept running through her mind. *Meet me at our bench in the park.* Furious over the assumption, she had refused. But then he'd warned her that if she didn't, he would ruin J.C. and Chrissy's futures. She couldn't imagine how, but she wasn't prepared to risk it.

Striding down the walk as though he owned it and every piece of land on either side, Owen arrived. He gestured toward the bench.

"I'll stand," she replied, unwilling to sit next to him. What, she wondered, had happened to the young man she once loved? Had these rotten seeds been in him all along?

Owen sent a proprietary gaze over the bench. "We spent a lot of afternoons here, talking about our future, planning our lives."

Anger dissolved into pity. "Owen, that was so long ago. We're different people now, too different."

"And J. C. Mueller isn't?"

"Why did you want to meet? You talked about his future and Chrissy's—"

"And yours. Maddie, I want to buy out your lease."

Puzzled, she stared at him.

"For your shop. I'll pay you twice what it's worth."

"I don't have a lease."

Owen frowned. "You rent the place month-to-month?"

"No. It's…" She paused, wanting to say it was none of his business, but she needed to know how he was threatening J.C. and Chrissy. "Why do you want to buy my lease?"

"Because I don't want you to lose your investment."

Truly baffled, she shook her head. "That won't happen. I don't want to hurt your feelings, Owen, but my shop, my business doesn't have anything to do with you."

"Even though I'm buying the Wagner Hill building?"

Shock struck hard and fast. "That's not true!"

"Why do think I paid off your account at the

costume shop? To keep you from going further in debt. You're probably not making enough in your tea parlor to cover costs."

Maddie shook her head, hating what she was hearing. "I'll pay back every cent."

"I can afford it. It'll be a write-off when the deal goes through for the building."

"I don't believe you."

"Ask J.C."

She knew J.C. wouldn't agree to Owen's deal. "Last night you said that if I didn't meet with you, it would ruin his and Chrissy's future. What did you mean?"

"I'm paying above market price, way above. You think anyone else would? That child can have an Ivy League education, then anything else she wants. J.C. knows a good deal when he sees it."

She couldn't speak.

"I have different plans for the Wagner Hill. Your tea parlor has to go."

"J.C. won't—"

"Grow up, Maddie. This is business, not personal."

But his tone told her it was. "I don't believe you."

Owen grasped her hand. "You're right, Maddie. We are different people now, better, stronger. You're the only woman I've ever loved."

Her throat was so choked she could barely speak. "I don't even know you anymore."

"You'll enjoy getting reacquainted."

She snatched her hand back. "No."

Satisfaction flooded his expression. "Face facts. You've rented out your mother's house. Your business and apartment will be gone. What then?"

Maddie shook with renewed anger.

"Accept it, Maddie. There's nothing you can do. Nothing."

Aimless and shaken, Maddie got in her car and drove. Owen had to be wrong. Malicious, but wrong. She turned into her old neighborhood, needing to get away from any of the more traveled streets. Tears burned in her eyes, clogged her throat.

Why had she agreed to meet Owen? To hear his lies?

She gripped the steering wheel. All she had to do was ask J.C. He... Would what? Tell her Owen had invented the story? But why would Owen lie about something so easily disproved? Unless it was true.

Maddie pictured J.C.'s face at dinner the previous night. Somber, strained, uncomfortable. And he couldn't get away fast enough once they had eaten. Just as he had avoided coming to dinner all week. She'd had no reason to question whether he genuinely had to work late each evening. Doctors had all kinds of crazy hours.

Reluctantly, she delved into her memory. Remembering, even though she didn't want to, that the week's hours weren't all that crazy. J.C. had arrived home every evening just late enough to be sure dinner was over.

The unwanted thoughts kept attacking. J.C. had to consider Chrissy's interests first. Maddie didn't resent that a bit. But to be speaking and dealing with Owen... To let Owen blindside her with the news...

Tears slid down her cheeks. It wasn't the loss of her shop that she was grieving. The Tea Cart was only one of her dreams. Disappointment wedged its way through her heart. Even though she had lectured herself not to, hope had been sprouting... making her wonder about a future with J.C. Even a family of her own.

She drove as though on autopilot until she turned onto her street, to the house she had grown up in, the house that was leased to another family for two years. Maddie had used the tenants' deposit to paint the exterior. It looked fresh, but not like home. Because it wasn't theirs again until the lease was up.

Maddie leaned her forehead against the steering wheel. How could J.C. have made a decision like this without talking to her? Pulling her home and business out from under her without a word?

Where would she and Mom live? And how would she pay for it? She had already committed the money from renting out their house to the roof contractor. She and her mother could have dealt with another season of catching leaks with buckets, but she couldn't expect renters to do the same.

But that paled next to how she felt. How she had hoped J.C. felt about her. Despite her responsibility for her mother, Maddie had thought perhaps it could be different with J.C. That he was different.

From what? she mocked herself. She'd been out of the dating game since her mother's first stroke. What did she know about men anymore? Worse, what had she ever known? If not for her mother's illness, she would be Mrs. Owen Radley. The thought made her stomach turn. Wrenched with pain, she tried to think of somewhere, anywhere to run to. There was only one place.

Ignoring the tears blurring her vision, Maddie drove until she reached Samantha's house. Praying her friend was home, she made herself look away from the gate leading to the backyard where they'd held the campout, where J.C. had almost kissed her.

"Hey! You should have called. I saw you driving up and remembered that we're out of coffee, and…" Samantha halted, stared, then hurried across the porch, wrapping Maddie in a hug. "What is it?" Samantha's voice choked. "Not your mother?"

"No, it's not Mom." Maddie allowed herself to be led inside.

Sam hovered, guiding her to the couch. "Do you want some…water?"

Shaking her head, Maddie swiped at her tears. Then she poured out the whole story. "I just can't believe it, Sam."

"Well, I *don't* believe it. What did J.C. say?"

"I haven't asked him."

"Why not?"

Tears and sobs exploded as though she had pulled a trigger.

"Oh, Maddie!" Sam rubbed her back for a few moments. Then she walked as fast as her cane would allow, bringing back a box of tissues. "I always say the wrong thing."

Maddie took a handful of tissues and leaned her face into it. When the worst of her crying jag ended, she pressed the knuckles of one hand to her lips to stop them from trembling. Taking a ragged breath, she looked at her friend. "It still seems unreal. I got the call from Owen last night..." She willed herself to not start crying again. "Then this morning when I met him..."

Sam stared at her in question.

"He said that J.C. and Chrissy's futures were at stake. I wouldn't have gone otherwise. Good thing I did."

"Good? Maddie, you've got to talk to J.C. He wouldn't do something like this. Certainly not without discussing it with you."

"It's our whole lives, Sam. Not just the shop, but we rented out our house..." She couldn't continue. *And she had given her heart to J.C.*

"You're talking crazy. No one's taking away your home and business. It was J.C.'s idea to back you. Why would he sell to a worm like Owen?"

"I told you—the money."

"No, not J.C."

"He has to think about Chrissy."

"And you." Sam face filled with concern and wisdom. "Don't you see it? He's nuts about you."

Maddie clapped a hand over her mouth, hoping to stop herself from crying. "Wishful thinking."

"Bret and I have both seen it. You two belong together."

"You know that's not possible. Besides, you don't do something like this to the person you love."

"Oh, Maddie, talk to him. Let him clear up whatever this is. Owen has cooked this up to try and get you back. The man has no principles!"

"Which says a whole lot about my judgment."

"Don't say that! You were too young to know what you do now, to see people for who they really are. At the same age, I thought my career was more important than Bret. I thank the Lord every day for the accident, for bringing me back to Him and to Bret."

"Apparently J.C. is no Bret, either."

Sam took her hands. "No. He's James Christopher Mueller. A fine man, a principled man of honor who cares about everybody he meets. He never gave up on me and I'm not going to let you give up on him."

Maddie bent her head, staring down, seeing nothing. "I keep coming back to the same thing. Why would Owen lie? He knows I can ask J.C."

"Maybe he hoped you wouldn't." Sam squeezed her fingers. "And it almost worked. You took the path of logic he hoped you would. Probably thought he could bluff his way through it."

"And what? That I wouldn't figure it out when the building didn't change hands?"

Sam hesitated.

"What?"

"It's possible Owen offered to buy Wagner Hill."

Maddie sucked in her breath. "Then it is all real."

"No, I didn't say that. Just that Owen could be trying to buy the building, to be in control."

"Control?"

"Of you, Maddie. Of you."

Knowing it must be done, Maddie steeled herself to talk with J.C. Actually, she would know just by J.C.'s demeanor if Owen had been telling the truth. J.C. didn't hide his feelings well. At least, she prayed he didn't.

J.C. sat by his patient's bedside. He had operated on her that morning and was optimistic about her recovery from a severe spinal injury. It was quiet in the intensive care unit. Her family had gone to the cafeteria after he assured them that she would sleep while they took a break.

He listened to the quiet but reassuringly steady rise and fall of her breathing, relieved that the procedure had gone well. J.C. had always felt comfortable at the hospital, it was his second home. One he was likely to need again soon. He had been waiting for Maddie to say something, to deny any involvement in Owen's plan. But there'd been nothing, no explanation.

"Doctor?" The nurse acknowledged his presence, then began recording his patient's vitals.

J.C. realized that this wasn't the place to do his thinking. With a nod, he left. The familiar scent of disinfectants was strong since an aide was mopping the floor. Glancing at his watch, J.C. realized it was almost midnight. He'd left a message on the answering machine to let Maddie know he would be late. Chrissy was no doubt asleep in the extra bed in Maddie's room. When she knew he wouldn't be home, Chrissy preferred to stay there close to the others. As much pain as he was in, J.C. couldn't begin to fathom how much it would hurt Chrissy to be yanked out of what she considered her home. When Maddie married Owen, the child wouldn't be part of her life any longer.

His office was quiet, dark. No one left soft lights on for him here. He flipped on the overhead fixture in the reception area, then switched on a lamp on his desk. Everyone had gone home to be with their families, tucked in safe and cozy.

The office was set up to be practical, not cozy. Accustomed to practical from years of being on his own, that had been fine with him. But it didn't exactly say welcome, sit and stay a while.

Sinking into his desk chair, he propped both

elbows on his desk and reached to open his laptop. But his hand fell away. Nothing it contained held any interest. Oh, there would be emails from college and med school friends, along with work that always needed to be done.

His fingers grazed the newspaper he had looked at earlier. The local Rosewood paper that was published twice a week was open to the small real estate section. He had circled ads for an apartment and a house. They would need something large enough for a live-in housekeeper and nanny. One that Chrissy would no doubt resent on sight. Truth was, with Maddie gone, he might as well sell the Wagner Hill. His niece's financial future would be secure and Owen's purchase would ensure that the site would never become a superstore.

Bending his head, J.C. rested it against his hands. *How had it come to this? How had he allowed this to happen again?* He was certain he had learned his lesson with his ex-wife. Knowing the signs of betrayal, he was sure they would never slip up on him again, that he would spot them immediately.

But Maddie had crept past all his defenses, made him trust again. *Lord, I am lost again.*

Feeling the Lord's urging, J.C. knew he would need every shred of his faith to make it through this time. Lifting his head, he swivelled his chair so that he looked out into the night. The only cars in the parking lot belonged to the staff and a handful of visitors. He hoped most of the visitors were new fathers staying the night with their wives and new babies, rather than relatives of critically ill patients.

J.C. remembered his plans for children, the vision he'd once had for a family. When they dated, Amy had assured him that she, too, wanted children. Meeting her near the end of medical school, she had seemed so sweet, so kind.

He swallowed. Much like Maddie. But that had changed after they were married. It was as though Amy had morphed into an entirely different person. Would that happen to Maddie? Was she wearing an assumed face? One that would change as soon as she and Owen married? The image scorched his already-tortured thoughts.

He remembered her many kindnesses, the deft touch she had with Chrissy. Instinctively, she had known not to try and step into Fran's place. Instead, she treated Chrissy like a favorite niece, and encouraged her bond with Lillian. How could she have faked that?

She didn't.

Was that the Lord's assurance or his own wishful longing?

The silence surrounding him didn't clarify which it was. Turning around, he stared out the doorway, the solitude reinforcing the emptiness of his life. It wasn't as bad during the day when he was surrounded by colleagues, staff and patients. But the nights…

Exhaling, he tried to close his mind to a lifetime of endless nights. Knowing there was only one thing that would help, he bent his head and prayed. And called on the Lord for help.

Chapter Eighteen

The Tea Cart's birthday party business for children had grown steadily since Chrissy's debut party. Now it was Lexi's birthday. Chrissy had pleaded to help host her best friend's big day. Maddie, still numb, would have agreed to almost anything for the child.

J.C.'s absences told her Owen hadn't lied. He stayed gone long into the nights, never home when he could run into her. Apparently he couldn't face telling her the truth.

Now, knowing Chrissy would also be out of her life, the hole in her heart deepened. She'd had a taste of what it would be like to have a child of her own. And she'd grown to love Chrissy, hoping she could help her past this worst time in her life, then watch her mature and grow into a young woman.

Hovering, Samantha clasped her elbow. "What is it?"

Maddie willed the shimmer of tears from her eyes. "Just thinking how fast kids grow up."

The expression on Samantha's face made it clear she knew there was far more, but she didn't press. "The cake and decorations are beautiful."

"Lexi's favorite color is pink. And I didn't want to repeat the gold." She tried desperately to focus on the setting, to take her thoughts away from herself...the pain.

"It's gorgeous. The tiaras are a nice touch."

"They were Chrissy's idea." Maddie smiled in spite of her distress. "And she insisted that we find one with pink and clear rhinestones for Lexi so it would be extra special. Tina ordered one that was a little larger than the others and switched out some of the clear rhinestones for pink."

"Chrissy's a sweet girl. Nice to see her that way again."

Swallowing around the lump in her throat, Maddie agreed. "She saved all of her allowance so she could buy Lexi a special birthday present." Maddie had contributed the difference so that Chrissy could buy the locket she wanted for her friend.

"Maddie, you haven't told me what J.C. said."

"Sam, he avoids me, doesn't come home until he's sure no one's still up. He has to let us know if he's going to be late so we can take care of Chrissy. But he makes sure he leaves a message on the answering machine so he doesn't have to talk to me."

"You mean you haven't asked him about Owen and the building?"

"There's not any point. I can tell by the way J.C. avoids me that Owen was telling the truth. Then, I was tidying up his apartment and saw..." Maddie drew in a ragged breath. "He had the real estate section of the paper next to his chair. He'd circled places to buy or rent."

"Could be any number of reasons..."

"Even you can't finish that statement." Maddie raised her gaze, seeing her friend's concern. "It's okay, Sam. I've always known I couldn't have a relationship anyway. Mom's my first priority."

"But J.C.—"

"Needs to move on. I've prayed about it, Sam. He has to do what's right for Chrissy."

"*This* is what's right for Chrissy. You've made a home for her, returned her ability to trust."

Maddie squinted against the pain. "She's given me the opportunity to know how it would be to have my own family. It's more than a fair trade."

Samantha stamped the foot of her good leg. "Maddie Carter, if you don't ask J.C. about the sale, I will."

"You can't."

"Oh, but I can. I'm not going to let you throw away your happiness because of pride."

"It's not pride." Maddie swallowed. "It's reality. You know, that bothersome fact that intrudes on stupid dreams."

"I want you to promise me that you'll talk to J.C., find out what's really going on with Owen."

"There's no point."

"Humor me," Sam implored. "I know this isn't right. It stinks of that rat. Don't let Owen ruin your future. You deserve more." She paused. "J.C. deserves more."

It wasn't a promise Maddie wanted to make. But Sam was only voicing what she had already decided. She did have to talk to J.C., if only to learn why.

And when her life would shatter.

The kids started arriving in the afternoon. Lexi had invited only girls. On the shy side, she preferred a princesslike tea party and didn't want the rowdier boys. Chrissy nearly popped waiting to show Lexi the special tiara with the sparkling pink and clear rhinestones. It looked perfect with the dainty pink dress Lexi's mother had sewn. Chrissy chose to wear one of the dresses that Tina had created for the Tea Cart. Maddie thought it was endearingly sweet that Chrissy didn't want to steal Lexi's spotlight by wearing her own special lavender birthday dress.

The other guests chattered nonstop as they picked out their dresses and popped on their tiaras. Maddie took mental snapshots, knowing she would never forget this day or the other days she had spent with Chrissy…with J.C.

Even though Maddie had baked a birthday cake, she also prepared tiny pink petits fours in the same pale pastel pink. Their *dress-up* tea party was touchingly sweet. All on their best behavior, the girls drank punch from teacups while wearing their petite white gloves.

Sam, along with Lexi's mother, helped Maddie serve. Lillian had opted to stay in her nook with two friends. Giggles resonated through the tea shop, causing the other few customers to smile. It was easy to imagine being ten years old again, having a fancy tea party with friends.

Concentrating on carrying in the birthday cake, Maddie didn't notice J.C. until she nearly slammed into him. He deftly stepped aside, preventing the crash. Flustered, she muttered an apology.

Glancing up, she caught the concern in his eyes. And...was that distress?

"Need help carrying that?"

Instinctively, she pulled the cake back. "No, I'm good. I'm fine."

He moved to clear the aisle, landing smack dab in front of the sketch of Maddie as a child at her teddy bear and doll tea party. His eyes lingered on the picture, then lifted to catch her gaze. Not so long ago, she would have grinned, shared the moment. Now all she could do was scurry away. If she stayed a moment longer the tears clogging her throat would escape.

Presenting the cake, she mouthed the words to

"Happy Birthday," as they all sang, hoping no one would notice. She wanted to be far away, hidden from prying eyes. She had no doubt that Sam would carry out her promise and talk to J.C. if she didn't. The possibility made her nearly faint with humiliation.

Maddie had tried to follow Sam's line of reasoning. Yes, it made sense that J.C. had never shown himself to be the same kind of person as Owen. But the silences, the avoidance. They weren't coincidental.

A huge part of her wanted to never broach the subject, like a child hiding beneath the covers on a stormy night. If she didn't ask, maybe it wouldn't happen. Equally childish.

Chrissy clapped when Lexi opened her present, the pink and silver cloisonné locket. Chrissy looked so happy, so content. And Maddie's resolve dissolved like ice on a hot summer's day. Chrissy deserved the best, everything she could possibly have in her future. She had already lost far more than any child should.

Maddie knew it was wrong for her to hope the building wouldn't sell. Jay had inherited the Wagner Hill from his parents. And although his printing business had done all right, it hadn't made a lot of money. Their home was saddled with a mortgage that about equaled its value.

Fran and Jay had an insurance policy, but nothing compared to what Owen was offering for the building. And who knew what would happen in the next eight years? Would there be enough money for Chrissy's education?

J.C. had poured a lot of cash into creating the Tea Cart. That must have dented his savings considerably. Guilt leached from every pore. While she'd worried about *her* future, *her* feelings, she hadn't really considered all the angles. Regardless of Owen's motives, his offer could change Chrissy's future. That was all that really mattered.

More giggles erupted from the children's corner. She would do whatever it took. And her heart would have to fend for itself.

Waiting through dinner seemed interminable. Chrissy was consumed with retelling every detail of Lexi's party. Her light chatter and Lillian's observations were all that could be heard. Each moment, Maddie wondered if J.C. might finally come home in time for dinner. But when they finished dessert, there was still no sign of him.

Chrissy helped her clear the table and load the dishwasher. Lillian was more than ready to retire by then. Although she had enjoyed watching the girls at the party, it had tired her. And she was more forgetful.

"Maddie, where do I sleep?"

"In your room, Mom. Just like always."

Lillian's eyes were vague. "Is this your house?"

"It's ours," she explained with a pang.

"I don't see my armoire." No, it had been too large to fit comfortably in the apartment, so it was in storage.

"I have your gown and robe." Maddie held them up.

"Good," Lillian murmured.

Maddie prayed that Lillian's worsening symptoms were temporary, only a result of fatigue, not signs of another small stroke. Casually, she reached for her mother's hand, clasping her wrist so that she could take her pulse. Thankfully, it was normal. Still, she uncapped the aspirin bottle and took out two pills. J.C. had told her if she suspected a stroke or heart attack, to give her mother two aspirins rather than one.

Scrutinizing her mother's moves, she saw that Lillian lifted her feet when she walked, a good sign. When it was a stroke, the person tended to drag their feet, unable to lift them properly.

"Mom, do you have a headache?"

"No, honey, I'm just tired."

Another good sign. Still, Maddie knew she had to call J.C. to be sure. She couldn't risk her mother's health.

Just then she heard footsteps in the hall. "Be right back, Mom." Dashing from her mother's room, she sped through the apartment, catching J.C. just before he entered his own place. "J.C."

He turned, looking surprised.

"It's probably nothing, but could you have a look at Mom? She's a little disoriented."

"Sure." Not making any small talk, he followed her back to Lillian's side.

He took her pulse and blood pressure, then checked her eyes with a pin light. "How are you feeling, Mrs. Carter?"

"Fine."

"Mom!"

"A little tired. Maddie's such a tattletale."

"She worries about you."

"That's because she's a good daughter." Lillian smiled tiredly at Maddie.

J.C. didn't reply, instead glancing at the pill case on the night stand. "Maddie, did you give her this morning's medicine?"

"Of course. I always…" The party, all the questions whirling in her thoughts… "I'm not sure."

He picked up the plastic container. "Today's meds are still here."

Maddie bit her lips. What a dumb trick. "I thought I had." She rubbed Lillian's back. "I'm sorry, Mom."

"Can I go to sleep now?"

"Of course." Maddie pulled the blanket up the way her mother liked. "All tucked in, snug as a bug in a rug." Kissing her forehead, Maddie inwardly thanked the Lord for watching over them, for not letting her mistake hurt her mother.

Maddie left the door ajar when they left the room

so she could hear if her mother needed anything, then walked with J.C. to the living room. "A few minutes ago I gave Mom two aspirins."

"She missed a dose of her blood thinner so that won't be a problem."

Rubbing her forehead, Maddie still couldn't believe she'd been so careless. "Thanks for checking on her."

"I suppose Chrissy's already asleep here."

Maddie hesitated. "When I didn't hear from you, I thought it was best."

"I was in surgery until late, then I tried to call but some of the lines must be down from the storm."

Blinking, Maddie realized that J.C.'s hair was wet, that some of the rain still dripped from his forehead, creasing his cheeks. She had been so concerned about her mother that she hadn't noticed anything else. "Storm?"

"Pretty wicked one. My coat's drenched." He wiped at the moisture on his bag. "Along with everything else."

"I haven't listened to the news. Didn't realize it's storming."

J.C. shrugged. "Not a good night to be out. Flash flood warnings are out for the whole area. Heard that on the car radio." He turned to leave just as a bolt of thunder hit close by.

"Um, speaking of news..."

He turned back, waiting.

Maddie fiddled with her hands, uncertain how to begin.

"News?" he prompted.

She swallowed. "Yours. News, I mean."

J.C. shook his head. "I don't know what you mean."

"I should have asked you when I spoke with Owen..." Glancing up, she saw J.C.'s jaw tighten, his eyes hardening. She took a deep breath. "He told me about the plans for the building, this building."

"Plans?" J.C.'s voice was dangerously tight.

"Yes, that he offered you a lot of money for it, that you plan to sell."

"It's what you want, isn't it?"

"Me?" Outraged, disbelieving, she wanted to shake him. "Of course. That's why I've worked myself to death, spent every penny I had to open the shop. Now you're pulling the rug out from under us. Or didn't it occur to you that when you sold the Wagner Hill you were also selling my home, my business?" She heard a small clatter, but before she could turn to look, J.C. grabbed her arm.

"*Your* home? What about my home?"

Baffled, hurt, overwhelmed, she stared at him. "I figured you must have plans for another home since you're selling this one to Owen."

"Says who?"

"Well...Owen." She narrowed her eyes. "Are you saying you didn't talk to him about selling the Wagner Hill?"

"I talked to him."

Maddie glowered, pain filling her very core. "But I didn't agree to sell the building."

"But he said—"

"I don't get it, Maddie. You're engaged to the man. His interests are yours."

"Engaged?" She flung her hands upward. "Years ago, when we were in college."

"You're not engaged now?"

She stared at him in amazement. "How can you even ask that? What engaged couple goes years without seeing each other?"

"How was I supposed to know that?"

"The fact that he never came around should have given you a clue."

J.C. stared into her eyes as though trying to read every particle of her thoughts. "I've seen you with him."

Frowning, Maddie tried to think. "He came to the shop on Chrissy's birthday."

"And you looked pretty cozy out on the sidewalk, and then again at the restaurant that Sunday."

"Cozy? Did you really say *cozy?*"

His lips were tight. "It sure looked that way."

"Then you're half blind. I hadn't seen Owen since we broke up. Then out of nowhere, he got all hot and bothered because I opened the Tea Cart."

"Without any encouragement?"

Anger joined her pain and her chest heaved with

suppressed fury. "I've never cross-examined your personal life."

"Not interested?"

"You don't get off that easily. I've given you room, respected what you want to keep private even when I…" Abruptly she halted before she could spill all of her feelings for him.

"When you what?"

Her breathing escalated, her stomach pitched. "Nothing."

J.C. took her hands. "Now *you* expect to get off that easily?"

"No, this can't happen."

"Maddie?" Lillian's fatigued voice barely reached the living room.

"I have to…"

J.C. gently squeezed her fingers. "We're not done."

Maddie sped to her mother's room. "What is it, Mom?"

"Chrissy. Find Chrissy."

"Mom, she's asleep in my room."

Lillian flopped her head from side to side, not lifting it from her pillow.

"I'll check on her real quick and be right back." Dying to finish her talk with J.C., Maddie was tempted to step out in the hall, then immediately return to her mother. But they'd never indulged in even small lies. Quietly, she entered her bedroom. Her own bed was still neatly made. She glanced at the other side of the room where Chrissy's bed was situated. It was empty. Apparently, she was in another room. Moving quickly, she checked out the bathroom connected to her room. Empty. She moved on to the second one. Also empty.

Chrissy must have wanted a snack, Maddie told herself. The light above the stove was on in the kitchen, but she didn't see anyone. Flipping on the overhead fixture, the light blared into every corner. Every empty corner. Maddie's breathing halted. The door from the kitchen that led to the outside hall was ajar.

J.C. followed the sound of her running from the rear of the apartment to the kitchen. "What's wrong?"

"Chrissy's not here, not in bed or any of the rooms." She pointed to the open door.

"She must have gone to her own room in our place." J.C. took the shortcut through the kitchen to the hall and into his apartment. Maddie was only steps behind him. Splitting up, they searched every room. Chrissy wasn't in any of them.

"Of course," Maddie exclaimed. "The leftover party favors are in the shop. She must be down there."

In sync, they rushed downstairs, turning on every light, but no giggling child emerged from the kitchen or the storeroom.

"J.C., where can she be?" A flash of lightning,

followed by a boom of thunder emphasized her words. "You don't think she's outside? In this storm?"

Striding to the front door, he grasped the doorknob and it turned easily. "Unlocked."

"She can't have gone far." Another flash of lightning illuminated the dark night sky.

J.C.'s face was grim. "She's a small child in a very large storm."

Maddie sucked in her breath. "We have to find her."

He flipped open his cell phone. "Tucker? J. C. Mueller. Chrissy's out in the storm somewhere. We're leaving now to look."

"The sheriff?" Maddie asked in a strangled voice.

"The more people looking means we find her faster." J.C. pulled open the door, Maddie on his heels. "You need to stay here with your mother."

"Give me your phone."

He obliged.

Maddie punched in Sam's phone number, filled her in quickly, then handed him back the phone. "She's on her way over and Seth will call volunteers to help look for Chrissy." She grabbed a coat from the rack by the door.

Stepping out onto the sidewalk, they were immediately assaulted by a lash of stinging rain. The gutters on Main Street were overflowing, rainwater rushing downhill, spilling over. The wind whipped the rain and hail into sideways slashes.

"Where would she go?" Maddie shouted.

J.C. turned his head, looking first up the street, then down. "Lexi's?"

Piling into his car, they drove as fast as the severely reduced visibility allowed. Lexi's father answered the door. They hadn't seen Chrissy but checked Lexi's room just in case. He and Lexi's mother offered to call the parents of other children in their class.

"Where now?" Maddie asked. Picturing Chrissy floating away in a massive surge of water, she bit back a sob. Not knowing when Chrissy left the apartment, they didn't know how far she could have traveled.

"Back to Main Street. She's on foot." He reversed the car and sped back to the center of town. The stores, bakery and café were all closed. A light was on at the bed and breakfast, but it wasn't a place Chrissy would go for refuge.

Refuge? Had Chrissy overheard them? Horrified, Maddie stiffened. "J.C, when you came upstairs, was the door from the kitchen to the hall open?"

"No."

Maddie closed her eyes. "She must have heard us."

"You said she was asleep."

Rain pounded on the car, hard, heavy, loud. "The storm. It must have woken her."

J.C. slammed his hand against the steering wheel.

"She thinks we're taking her home away, that things will be the same as they were before…"

Their eyes met.

Before they had come together as a family.

"Oh, J.C., we have to find her!"

He stared into the ominous night. Then he jerked the car back into gear, driving down Main Street.

Maddie didn't know where he was headed, but she had faith in him. She placed her ultimate faith in the Lord's hands, beseeching Him to watch over Chrissy, to allow them to find her, to bring her safely home. To their home.

J.C. turned, driving in a sharp, short burst. Screeching to a sudden stop, J.C. put the car in Park and yanked up the emergency brake.

Maddie jumped from the car, barely able to see where they were. Recognizing the town cemetery, she gasped.

J.C. didn't hesitate, striding past the front gate. Maddie kept even with his pace. Sure-footed, he cut through the rows, heading for what must be familiar. Because the rain was pounding relentlessly, obscuring their vision, rendering everything to a seemingly different state, nothing looked as it should.

Not ceasing her prayers, Maddie dogged his lead, afraid she'd lose sight of him, more afraid that they wouldn't find Chrissy.

Reaching one of the outer sections, J.C. finally

stopped. Maddie took another step so she could stand even with him.

Huddled against the Mueller family headstone, Chrissy clung to the engravings of her parents' names on the stone, sobbing.

J.C. reached her first, scooping Chrissy up into his arms, pressing her against his chest, shielding her as best as he could from the relentless downpour. "What are you doing here?"

Chrissy sobbed even harder.

Maddie wiped at the water that drenched her small face, her sodden clothing. "Oh, sweetheart, we were so worried."

Unable to speak, Chrissy flung her head from side to side in denial.

"I love you, Pinker Belle," J.C. told her.

"Me, too," Maddie added, wishing she could take back everything the child had heard, return her hard-won security.

Rain pelted the child's stricken face. "Then why is everyone leaving?"

J.C. met Maddie's gaze. "No one's going anywhere."

"I heard you!" Chrissy accused, raw pain filling each word.

"I'm not selling the building," J.C. reassured her. "We're still going to live in our apartment."

"What about Maddie?"

Again J.C. caught her gaze. "That's up to Maddie."

Chrissy fixed her imploring gaze on Maddie.

"Sweetheart, you're part of my life, Mrs. Lillian's life." Praying her words would be true, she touched Chrissy's cheek. "That's not going to change."

J.C. caught Maddie's eyes, locking them in a challenge, a promise.

"Let's get you home," he told his niece. "Home."

Chapter Nineteen

With the same sure direction, J.C. took them back through the cemetery, depositing Chrissy in the backseat of his SUV. He grabbed a blanket from the rear and draped it over her trembling body. Turning on the heater, he drove quickly but not frantically back home.

As soon as they were inside, Maddie took over, guiding Chrissy into a warm bath, then getting her dressed in warm flannel pajamas. While she did, J.C. made hot cocoa. Maddie arched her eyebrows when she saw that he had.

"Hidden talents," he explained while Maddie wrapped Chrissy in a warm blanket.

They took their places on either side of Chrissy on the sofa, while she cautiously sipped her cocoa. Exhausted, emotionally drained, she leaned her head on J.C.'s strong shoulder. Maddie smoothed the child's drying hair, incredibly grateful that she was all right, that they had found her before the storm could sweep her away.

Chrissy handed her uncle the mug, unable to finish her cocoa. With her free hand, she reached for Maddie's hand and clung on.

Tears stung Maddie's eyes. Tears of gratitude and love.

"Do you promise we'll always be together?" Chrissy asked.

"I promise you'll always be with me," J.C. replied.

Maddie pushed away the dart of pain. He hadn't included her.

"Together," Chrissy said, her voice sleepy.

"Together," J.C. echoed.

Chrissy's eyelids drooped, then drifted shut. Carefully, J.C. eased off the sofa so that he could prop Chrissy's head on the armrest and allow her to stretch out.

"Do you want to take her home?" Maddie asked.

"I want to keep an eye on her tonight. I can't sleep anyway."

Maddie tucked the blanket closer, then reluctantly rose, following J.C. into the kitchen. Again switching roles, he turned on the electric kettle and reached for two cups. A canister of tea sat on the small breakfast table. But she didn't feel like sitting. Or drinking tea.

J.C.'s voice remained even. "Do you still love him?"

Maddie wanted to scream, flail, pound the wall.

All too aware of Chrissy and her mother, she couldn't. Tears smarted, but she refused to give in to them. "How can you even ask that?"

"Because I have to know." He no longer looked forbidding.

"Of course I don't."

"And what about me?"

Tears tortured her eyelids, flooded her voice. "You're a man who deserves a loving wife who can devote everything to her family."

J.C. stepped closer. "And what do you deserve?"

Helplessly she held open her hands.

Taking one more step, he smoothed her hair back over one shoulder. "What do you want?"

Tears snuck out, one by one. "It's not about what I want. I am going to take care of Mom, that won't ever change."

"Of course not," he replied calmly.

She bit her lip. "But until you meet the right woman, I'm where I want to be."

"I've met her." He cupped her chin. "*You're* the right woman."

Irony was like a sword to her throat. "Afraid not. Mom and I come as a package deal."

"So?" J.C. stroked her cheek, savoring the softness of her skin.

"So I can't be that right woman, the one who can devote herself completely to you."

"Funny, I don't remember writing that on my application." His upturned lips were close to hers. "I believe I asked for the woman with the largest heart in the world, who can love her mother, an orphaned child and if I'm very, very lucky, me."

Heart quaking, she felt his breath mingle with hers. "You deserve more—"

He placed two fingers on her lips, hushing her words. "I don't deserve you, Maddie Carter, but I love you. I think I fell in love with you the first day you walked into my office."

Her eyes searched his. "I'll never put Mom in a home."

"Not even ours?"

Breath stuttering, she tried to control her tears.

Gently, he smoothed each drop from her cheeks. "We're a family, Maddie. We might not have planned it that way, but we are, and I wouldn't trade one member for anything in the world."

"I can't believe…"

"Believe."

She traced the outline of his strong jaw. "Did I tell you that I love you?"

His eyes said it all, the gold flecks reflecting each unspoken word.

"I love you, J.C. With all my heart, with every breath I take."

That breath caught as he touched his lips to hers, possessive, loving, completing. And Maddie knew it was for real.

* * *

Hammers and electric saws pounded and buzzed; Sheetrock dust and wood shavings littered the floors. Ripping down the exterior walls between the apartments had been J.C.'s idea. Maddie suggested an arched opening for the connection. And Seth found the perfect spot for the exterior door just past the head of the stairs. With some reconfiguring, he was able to create an entry hall, and fashion the two living areas into a den and living room. J.C.'s old bedroom became Lillian's new room, right next to Chrissy's, which pleased both of them immensely. The wall between Maddie's bedroom and Lillian's old one was shifted so they would have a larger master bedroom with an adjoining smaller space perfect for a future nursery.

They were able to stay in the apartments until it was time to alter the bedrooms. Sam and Bret opened their home, inviting them all to stay until the work was done. Seth had a strict deadline. Their new unified home had to be completed by the time they arrived back from their honeymoon.

J.C. offered Maddie the world. She chose Paris. Not having traveled outside Rosewood since college and never having left the United States, Maddie had vacationed in her mind, exploring the Louvre and Musée d'Orsay, walking the banks of the Seine, gazing at the Eiffel Tower, strolling beneath the Arc de Triomphe. Now, she would retrace those imaginary steps with her groom.

Initially, she worried about leaving Lillian and Chrissy for two weeks. But practically everyone in Rosewood stepped up, offering to help. Familiar with the shop, Sam would run the Tea Cart. Chrissy and Lillian would keep to their normal routine, then spend evenings with Samantha and Bret. Each and every one of Maddie's protests was shot down, made null and void.

J.C. took care of her primary concern, telling Owen that he would never sell him the Wagner Hill. Not long afterward, J.C. was contacted by the superstore Owen had intended to build on the site once the Wagner Hill was demolished. The entire plan exposed, and realizing that Maddie was really going to marry J.C., Owen left Rosewood for Dallas where his family's corporate headquarters were located.

Maddie was filled with relief. Not that she had much time to worry anyway. Caught up in wedding preparations, every hour was full to the brim. Emma insisted on designing the wedding gown, but she didn't have to do much persuading.

Still, on the big day, Maddie touched the silk confection reverently. "Emma, it's too beautiful to wear."

Accustomed to dealing with brides, Emma took the comment in stride. Still, her smile was soft. "It's not nearly as beautiful as you are."

"Ditto," Samantha chimed in.

"Maddie is the most beautiful woman in the world," Lillian declared, then patted Chrissy's knee. "And I've got the most beautiful *girl* in the world right next to me."

The sweetness that perfumed the bride's room had little to do with the scattered rose petals and everything to do with the bond between the occupants. It was as smooth as the silk that settled over Maddie's hips, then trailed to cover her bare toes and puddle like a swirl of icing. Long sleeves of soft, delicate lace came to perfect pyramids on each hand. The same lace fitted around her neck and shadowed the silk bodice. Tiny pearls were hand sewn on the waist. The same pearls festooned the veil that flared down her back to trail behind the full-skirted dress.

Samantha clasped her chest. "Oh, my. Maddie…"

Carefully, slowly, Maddie turned to the full-length mirror. "It's this incredible dress."

"Every time she makes one, I think it's the most gorgeous ever," Samantha murmured. "And it is."

"But it's the bride wearing it that makes the dress beautiful," Emma insisted. "You are an exquisite bride, but then I expected nothing less."

"Ditto," Samantha muttered, wiping at a tear.

"Honestly, Samantha, you have become the soggiest, most romantic person I know." Maddie sniffled.

Emma softly clapped her hands together. "Makeup, ladies. We're all be reapplying if you two don't stop." She glanced at her watch. "Chrissy, it's time for you and Mrs. Lillian to take your places."

While Chrissy wheeled Lillian to the vestibule, Samantha helped Emma adjust the veil so that it fell perfectly over Maddie's loose curls that were softly gathered in an upsweep. "I feel like I'm sending my child out into the world!" Samantha wailed.

"Knowing the kind of friend you are, you'll be a great mom someday."

"Glad you think so." Samantha patted her slim stomach. "Someday's arrived. A few more weeks and Emma would have had to let out my dress."

"Oh, Sam!" Forgetting about her dress or makeup, she pulled her matron of honor into a hug. Sam and Bret had been hoping for some time. "I'm so happy for you."

"You crush Maddie's dress and I'll wish twins on you," Emma threatened.

They all laughed.

Wiggling her bare feet, Maddie slipped on her shoes. "I think that's it."

"Perfect," Emma declared.

"Are you ready?" Samantha asked.

"Oh, yes." She had been ready since the moment J.C. proposed.

Emma opened the wide double doors. Organ music floated from the sanctuary. Now the scent of roses did permeate the air. As a botanist, Samantha had lovingly helped Maddie choose the perfect flowers. They agreed that white roses suited the innate beauty of the aged sanctuary. Nestled among them were exquisite hand-chosen orchids.

But Maddie wanted her bouquet to be a declaration of her love. Flawless scarlet roses. The eternal symbol of love, her love for the man not only of her dreams, but who had made her dreams a reality.

Anxious to see J.C., to begin their new life together, Maddie practically floated to the archway that opened onto the center aisle of the sanctuary. There, waiting to give her away, were Lillian and Chrissy.

Lillian grasped Maddie's elbow, which would ensure she was steady as they walked to the alter. "I know you'll be as happy as your father and I were."

"Oh, Mom." Maddie kissed her cheek.

Chrissy tugged at the waist of her chiffon dress made of the palest of lavenders. She and Lillian, as well as Samantha, wore the same color, their dresses a delicate blush of lavender with just enough color to accent Maddie's gown.

Samantha squeezed Maddie's fingers. "Be happy, my friend." Despite her cane, her steps were even as she proceeded up the aisle, holding a nosegay of white roses.

"Ready?" Emma asked.

Maddie smiled. "Absolutely."

Emma signaled the organist and the familiar notes of the wedding march trumpeted through the sanctuary. With her mother and Chrissy on either side, Maddie felt as though her feet didn't even touch the ground as she walked toward her groom.

Tall, achingly handsome, he was dressed in a black tuxedo and crisp white shirt. The boutonniere he had chosen was also a scarlet rose, one that matched hers. His eyes lit up as he caught sight of her and didn't waver, holding hers as she came to stand beside him.

The pastor began the age-old words, soon asking, "Who gives this woman?"

Lillian and Chrissy chorused, "We do."

Chrissy held Lillian's hand as they sat in the reserved pew.

Gazing at J.C., Maddie wanted to pinch herself, to believe this wonderful man was to be her husband. The pastor's words spilled over her like polished diamonds on velvet.

"Do you take…"

"In sickness and health…"

"Until death do us part."

"I do," Maddie vowed.

J.C. echoed her response.

"I now pronounce you husband and wife."

Their lips met, a gentle kiss of promise. An overture of love flooded them both.

J.C. took Maddie's hand, holding it as though he would never let it go. "Are you ready, Mrs. Mueller?"

A love so overpowering it filled every particle, every pore, sang through her veins. "Are *you* ready, Mr. Mueller?"

J.C. drew her hand to his lips, kissing it softly. "Only for the next fifty years or so."

Music poured from the organ, guiding their first married steps as they traveled down the aisle and into the future created from faith and love, their own family by design.

* * * * *

Dear Reader,

Sometimes a book comes from the whisper of an idea or from experience. In an ever-shifting world, I draw from both. I was blessed with loving, caring parents. The immeasurable bond between my mother and myself was a gift from the Lord. Even when dementia robbed her memory, her love for me never wavered. I am thankful every day for what we shared and how incredibly blessed I was to have her for my mother.

I always wished to have the same relationship with my own daughter, but when "she" was born, it was a boy! Brian has been an incredible blessing and this last year had his first child, a baby girl, Liberty. She's only the third girl in five generations of my family! A miracle! My daughter-in-law, Lindsey, is my girl now, too, a true daughter who I love.

The Lord knew I always wanted a sister, so He gave me friends who are my sisters. Through one, Karen, I was blessed with the daughter of my heart, Erica. She has been dear to me since she was a child, and with her I have been able to have the mother-daughter relationship that I prayed for.

I've never known if life does indeed imitate art, but I do know that we are all incredibly fortunate to have families, whether they're of our blood or not, who care about and love us. My wish for you, dear reader, is that your life is blessed with family, perhaps even family by design.

God bless,

Bonnie K. Winn

Questions for Discussion

1. Because of Maddie's decision not to put her mother in a nursing home, she lost the man in her life. Would you have done the same thing as Maddie, or made a different decision. Why or why not?

2. Nine-year-old Chrissy experienced an unexpected and profound loss when both her parents died. How do you think Chrissy was handling the loss? What about J.C.?

3. Did you agree with J.C.'s solution to finding Chrissy a secure home?

4. After seeing that they could both help each other, J.C. offers a solution to their situations. If you were Maddie, would you have accepted the solution, or would you have gone a different way?

5. Have you ever had a relationship with someone not born into your family, but who feels that way? Please explain.

6. Just when Maddie's dream of opening a tea shop is becoming reality, her ex-boyfriend Owen comes back into her life, acting strangely.

Do you think Maddie should have tried to learn more about the man Owen had become?

7. Do you think that J.C. jumped to conclusions about Maddie's relationship with Owen too quickly? What could he have done differently to save them both heartache?

8. Chrissy and Lillian seem to get along very well. Why do you think that is?

9. Maddie had given up many of her life's dreams and goals to care for her mother. Which dream do you think became most important to Maddie? Why or why not?

10. Maddie eventually finds out who's been trying to ruin her plans for her tea shop—and her "family." Have you ever experienced betrayal by a loved one? A friend? How did it turn out for you?

11. If you were J.C., would you have sold the Wagner Hill building? Did you agree with J.C.'s decision? Explain.

12. Did you feel that J.C. and Maddie had the basis for a strong marriage? Do you think they will have a "happily-ever-after"?

LARGER-PRINT BOOKS!

**GET 2 FREE
LARGER-PRINT NOVELS
PLUS 2 FREE
MYSTERY GIFTS**

Love Inspired

Larger-print novels are now available...

LILP11B